Absence Makes the Heart Grow Fondant

Baker's Rise Mysteries

Book Three

R. A. Hutchins

Copyright © 2021 Rachel Anne Hutchins

All rights reserved.

The characters, locations and events portrayed in this story are wholly the product of the author's imagination. Any similarity to any persons, whether living or dead, is purely coincidental.

Cover Design by Molly Burton at cozycoverdesigns.com

ISBN: 9798773047315

For Hopey Doodle
Who will be an author herself one day!

Love you to the moon and back
And all around the stars 🌙

xxx

CONTENTS

If you follow this list in order, you will have made a perfect
Traditional Christmas Cake *to enjoy while you read!*

1)	**How to make the perfect Christmas cake**	**1**
2)	**Find your most festive apron!**	**9**
3)	**List of ingredients:**	**17**
4)	1kg (5 cups) Mixed Dried Fruit	25
5)	Zest and juice of 1 orange and 1 lemon	34
6)	250g (1 ¼ cup) butter, softened	41
7)	200g (1 cup) soft light brown sugar	50
8)	150ml (½ to 1 cup) brandy or other alcohol plus extra for feeding	58
9)	175g (1 cup) plain flour	66
10)	100g (½ cup) ground almond	74
11)	½ tsp baking powder, 2 tsp mixed spice, 1 tsp ground cinnamon, ¼ tsp ground cloves	82
12)	100g (½ cup) flaked almonds	89
13)	4 large eggs	97
14)	1 tsp vanilla extract	104
15)	Put dried fruit, citrus juices and zests, alcohol, butter and brown sugar in a large pan	111
16)	Set over a medium heat. Bring to the boil, then lower the heat and simmer for 5 mins.	118
17)	Tip the fruit mixture into a large bowl and leave to cool for 30 mins.	126
18)	**Heat oven to 150C/130C fan/gas 2**	**135**
19)	Line a deep 20cm cake tin with a double layer of baking parchment, then wrap a double layer of newspaper around the outside – tie with string to secure	142

20) Add flour, ground almonds, baking powder, mixed spice, cinnamon, cloves, flaked almonds, eggs and vanilla extract to the fruit mixture and stir well   152

21) Tip into your prepared tin, level the top and bake in the centre of the oven for 2 hrs.   160

22) Put your feet up with a hot drink and a cosy book!   168

23) Remove the cake from the oven, poke holes in it with a skewer and spoon over 2 tbsp of your chosen alcohol. Leave the cake to cool in the tin   176

24) To store, peel off the baking parchment, then wrap well in plastic wrap   183

25) Feed the cake with 1-2 tbsp alcohol every 2 weeks, until you ice it.   189

26) Don't feed the cake for the final week to give the surface a chance to dry before icing.   198

27) Cover with Marzipan, and Fondant icing, and then Decorate.   205

28) Enjoy a happy holiday season!   210

Baker's Rise Mysteries Book Four   219
About The Author   221
Other books by this Author   223

ONE

The first week of November made its presence felt with rain, lots of rain, the kind that soaks through your clothes within minutes, leaving everyone looking bedraggled and feeling irritable. By week two, even Reggie was sick of it, happy to travel between the tearoom and the coach house in his little carrier case to avoid the downpour. Flora herself was feeling exhausted, and spread rather too thinly between her various projects, though she would never admit as much. She knew she had only herself to blame – after all, what sane person would try to build up a small tearoom business, embark on a career as a children's author, begin renovations on a huge manor house and also convert another part of the stable block at the same time?

Well on the way to a full recovery following her hip surgery, the only evidence of which was a walking stick which the woman used only reluctantly, Betty had just finished giving Flora her rather vocal views on the subject of Flora's many projects. It was spoken from a place of love and concern, Flora knew, but nevertheless still slightly annoying. The older woman had been quick to point out Flora's huge grey bags under her eyes, her tightly-drawn features and her inability to sit still for more than five minutes at a time. She was quite right of course, and said nothing that Flora didn't already know herself. Pouring them both another cup of Earl Grey, Flora tried to subtly change the subject, to one that she knew was close to Betty's heart.

"So, Betty, tell me more about this cruise that you and Harry have booked for the middle of November through to December. It's to the Caribbean, did you say?" Flora knew fine well that the couple were cruising the Caribbean for a whole month – in fact she thought she could probably recite their whole itinerary by heart if pushed, she had been told so many times! She didn't mind, though, as Betty's enthusiasm was contagious, and Flora could pretty much just tune out of the conversation and run through her 'to do' list in her mind. She had finally finished sorting through

Harold's paperwork in the big house last month, so the electricians and heating engineers had been hard at work rewiring and installing whole new plumbing systems, whilst a team of roofers were patching up the worst of the damage. Once these were all complete, the main refurbishment and redecoration could begin, though this would be slowed as Flora's finances were unfortunately not as healthy as her imagination. Despite this, unable to face the prospect of sorting through the deceased man's bedroom, Flora had plans to hire a house clearance company in the new year to go through the two upper floors of The Rise, though the decision of what was to be done with the furniture and other items they had found would still be Flora's to make. Flora felt it would be worth every penny!

Not for the first time, Flora was grateful that her years spent with her ex-husband Gregory, both of them working flat out in the City, had at least afforded her a decent divorce settlement. Gregory had insisted on keeping their ridiculously large house in Kensington, with his latest paramour, which meant that he had had to buy Flora out of her share in the building, though that money seemed to be very slow in coming. Harry had chased Gregory's solicitors a few times for the house settlement, but had received nothing more tangible than vague reassurances in reply. When that money did finally materialise, it would be added to the manor house pot. Flora was confident that, provided she was frugal and didn't go overboard, she could complete the majority of the work she needed to. The income from the estate would keep things running once her savings had set everything up. Whether she would live in The Rise next year, when enough rooms had been made liveable, Flora wasn't sure, as she loved her little home in the converted coach house.

"Don't you think, lass?" Betty looked rather irritated, as if it wasn't the first time she'd asked.

"Sorry, Betty, could you repeat the question?"

"I knew it! I knew your mind was running a mile a minute again!"

"I'm so sorry, Be…"

"It's not your apologies I want, lass, I just need to know that you're not running yourself into the ground. And when's this racket going to stop?" Betty indicated the direction of the wall behind them, soon to be knocked through to the other stable block which was currently being renovated into a bookshop and little library.

"Yes, they are rather loud today, sorry about that. I'm

closing the tearoom next week so that they can knock through the wall and finish it all off. Adam has taken a few days' leave from work to help me with the painting and putting in the book shelves."

"Well, it all sounds lovely, don't get me wrong, I think what you're doing for the village is grand, but it's a lot to carry on one set of shoulders that's all," Betty rubbed Flora's arm affectionately, "then there'll be that Christmas talent show you've agreed to organise while Pepper and George Jones are away – Baker's Rise Stars in their Eyes."

"I know, I know, I'll definitely need to get more regular help when the bookshop's all open, though Tanya's been great for the odd morning here and there in the tearoom. I may see if she would like something more permanent," Flora mused, her brain whirring again.

"Aye well, make sure you do! Now, don't forget you said you would come round on Saturday so that I could share my Christmas cake recipe with you. It's old Granny Lafferty's with her secret ingredient, so not to be shared with anyone else though!" the older woman warned with a wink as she stood to leave.

"My lips are sealed!" Flora promised, as Reggie flew over to her shoulder and nuzzled into her. Betty lifted

Tina the Terrier into her lap and the two animals eyed each other warily. Thankfully, after the pair had teamed up to distract Emma Blenkinsopp when Betty and Flora had both worked out that she was guilty of Ray Dodds' murder, they seemed to have formed a truce. Reggie no longer screeched, "Tina the Terror," whenever he saw the little dog, and she didn't feel the need to cower under the table. It made for much more peaceful visits all round!

The sound of Harry's car pulling up outside, come to collect Betty, interrupted their conversation. When Betty opened the door to brave the elements, her head wrapped in a scarf and then a rain hood, all under her big umbrella and with Tina under her other arm, a gust of wind and wetness blew in causing Flora to shiver. Reggie moved to hide beneath the flap of the tartan scarf she wore indoors to keep the chill at bay. The central heating wasn't very good in the tearoom, so Flora was having another couple of radiators installed when the place was closed the following week. Waving goodbye to Betty from the window, Flora gathered the dirty cups and plates from the table, wondering if she should just pop next door and see how they were faring. In the end, she decided against it, as she had already called in twice that day, and she could tell that Ted Charlton and his crew were getting slightly sick of her overly-regular visits!

Instead, Flora washed the dishes, then took her trusty notebook from her apron and began to add more jobs to her 'to do' list. Her new reading glasses, which she had finally managed to get, were perched on her nose. Flora didn't much like wearing them in public, feeling that they aged her considerably, but when it was just her and Reggie she was happy to not have to squint to get things in focus. Although her list was long, and getting longer by the day, in fact, she was starting to move away from the conversion and refurbishment and instead to focus on kitting out the book shop. This was the part Flora was most looking forward to! She planned on getting young Aaron and the Marshall girls in to help her look through book catalogues and to give her their suggestions for children's books, and then Amy from the hairdressers had been very keen to give Flora some suggestions for more adult reads. Besides that, though, Flora planned to have a sign-up sheet at the tearoom, and one on the church notice board, for any of the villagers to suggest books for either the shop or the small library corner. She was still to work out how the lending and borrowing system for the little library would work, but Flora had it near the end of her 'To Do' list and hoped things would become clearer once she actually had the books in.

Aaron was finally starting to come out of his shell again since his Grandad's death, and everyone – Flora included – was relieved to see it. For a while, when he and mum Shona had moved back into the pub, the Bun in The Oven, he had been quiet and withdrawn. Shona had confided in Flora that both she and her son had visited a grief counsellor, and thankfully the boy was now slowly starting to seem more like his old self. The pub still hadn't reopened, and Flora had given Shona a six-month rent holiday to help her get back on her feet, with plans that there would be a Grand Reopening of the establishment over Christmastime. The locals were missing their social hub, but it had had the knock-on effect that more people were coming to the tearoom for their catch-ups! So, Flora couldn't complain.

In fact, she had very little to complain about – being busy wasn't necessarily bad, and it was for such a short space of time in the grand scheme of things. If nothing else happened to tip the boat, then Flora was sure she could handle everything. Though, she herself had to admit, that was a pretty big 'if.'

TWO

Flora had just taken off her rain-soaked coat and boots, unwound her outdoor scarf from around her neck, and laid them all over the radiator in the hallway of the coach house to dry, when the doorbell rang. Reggie squawked unhappily, still shut as he was in his travel case, so Flora moved to unlatch the little flap and set him free. Expecting it to be Ted Charlton, come to give her the day's recap of his team's progress – he didn't like to come into the tearoom in his work gear – Flora pulled the door open whilst simultaneously bending to the small hallway table to release Reggie. As she straightened up, Flora was almost knocked off balance again by the sight of the man who stood in front of her. Far from being the friendly builder, it was her ex-husband, Gregory, whom she now faced for the first time in many months.

Almost too stunned to speak, Flora stood gawking at the man. Her first instinct was to check if her bobbed hair lay smoothly and to try to remember how recently she had applied any make-up – old habits die hard, and Gregory had always expected her to look a certain way – until Flora checked herself. She really didn't care what he thought of her any more. She would dress how she chose, and couldn't even recall when she had last seen her make-up bag.

In return, and apparently unable to help himself, Gregory looked Flora up and down, the disapproval in his gaze all too clear until he masked it behind a façade of cheery reacquaintance. Flora ran her hands over her thick knitted cardigan (a handmade gift from Jean in Baker's Rise Essential Supplies) and met his stare. Gregory himself looked pristine in a designer suit and overcoat. Even his umbrella had the small insignia of an expensive brand.

"Flora, I'm so happy I found you! You couldn't get any more out in the sticks, could you?" he chuckled, but it was an empty sound. The wind swept past them both and into the small hallway, making Flora want to slam the door to preserve what little heat there was inside her home at this time of day. The central heating wouldn't click on from its timer on the thermostat for another half an hour yet.

"Couldn't you have phoned?" Flora asked bluntly. There was no love lost between she and her ex-husband, so she saw no point in pretending there was.

"Well, I, I mean, I was hoping to see you in person, Flo, I've missed you. Argh!" Gregory let out a sudden shriek as he was divebombed by a shiny green parrot and Flora struggled to contain the giggle that rose up her throat, "What the heck is that?"

"It's Flora," he'd lost the right to use that little nickname a long time ago, "and that's Reggie! He has a good sense for whom to like and who... not to – unless you're a beautiful young woman selling sweets," Flora added, watching in secret pleasure as Reggie flapped his wings around Gregory's head, messing his perfect comb-over.

In the end, she decided to take pity on the man, "Enough, Reggie, calm or cage!" and waited as the bird came back to her own shoulder, for once giving a surprising impression of being perfectly trained! "I'm surprised to hear that you've missed me. I would've thought you'd be busy enough with work and... what was her name? Sherry? Chardonnay"

"Ginny."

"Ah yes, I knew it had an alcoholic connection. That's

why I just drink the tonic water these days, or, better still, stick to wine," Flora added sardonically.

"Yes, well, we're no longer together. I've come to my senses, you might say, and I wanted you to be the first to know."

"Me? Whatever for?" Flora was genuinely perplexed by the sudden appearance.

"Well, I hoped we might…"

"Alright, Flora, sorry to interrupt, just got the day's update," Flora had never been so glad to hear Ted Charlton's voice from behind Gregory. Obviously she couldn't keep the man waiting, standing as he was in the pouring rain.

"Thank you, Ted, my guest is just leaving," she said pointedly, looking her ex squarely in the eyes.

"Oh, well, couldn't I just wait insi…?"

"I'm afraid not!" Flora interrupted Gregory quickly, before he could make any ludicrous suggestions such as coming inside for a cuppa and a catch up! "Reggie gets very twitchy when we have strangers in the house!"

Gregory turned on his heel, the muscle in the side of

his temple twitching – a sign, Flora knew, that his anger was barely restrained and was about to boil over. *Not my problem*, she thought, gratefully, and instead moved her attention to Ted. They began speaking, as the tyres on Gregory's latest edition BMW shrieked on the gravel, spinning as he tried to reverse away too fast for the conditions.

"Sorry about that," Flora said, smiling on the outside, but still a little shocked on the inside.

"Aye, strange bloke," Ted observed, "obviously not from the area."

"No, definitely not," Flora agreed, keen to then change the subject back to her new bookshop and put all thoughts of unwelcome exes out of her mind.

Finally in her armchair, with the log burner giving out a pleasing amount of heat to warm her freezing toes, Flora sat back with a sigh. She really had no idea what that had all been about with Gregory, but she knew her ex-husband too well to think that she'd seen the last of him. No, when Gregory got something in his head, particularly when it was something he wanted, then he would stop at nothing to get it. The thought chilled Flora right through, as if the cold had suddenly travelled north from her feet and up through her whole body. She shivered and pulled the plaid throw from the couch across her lap. Reggie looked at her inquisitively from his perch opposite, for a moment pausing his contented chirping.

"Good bird," Flora said, as much to reassure him as to make sure her own voice sounded normal. She was rather more shaken than she'd like to admit.

"My Flora," Reggie replied, flying over and landing on her lap.

Flora stroked his head absentmindedly as she considered whether she should call Adam to tell him of this new development in her life. October had been such a quiet month – busy but uneventful – and Flora had dearly hoped that it would stay that way right up until Christmas. The decision was taken out of her hands, however, when the phone next to her began to ring and Adam's name flashed up on the display.

"Great minds!" Flora said as she answered.

"Eh?"

"I was just thinking of calling you," she explained.

"Oh, well, that's perfect then. How are you doing, love? I'm on duty but there's not much going on tonight, so I thought I'd give you a quick call!"

"That was very thoughtful. I'm fine."

"You don't sound fine, if you don't mind me saying. In fact, it's been quite a few weeks since I've heard your voice without your usual enthusiasm. Has something happened?"

Flora explained about her rather random visitor, hearing Adam's sharp intake of breath as she mentioned her ex-husband.

"But he's definitely gone now? And you've locked the door with that new bolt I put on?" Adam asked, clicking into police mode as he often did, Flora noted.

"Yes, I saw him drive away. But to be honest, I doubt he's left the area. If he wants something, he'll stay until he gets it."

"And what do you think that something could be?" Adam asked.

"Well, he says it's me, but that's hardly a likely story. Knowing Gregory, it'll be to do with money."

"But the divorce is final."

"I know, I really don't have any idea…" Flora exhaled loudly.

"Sorry love, I didn't mean to give you twenty questions. I'll pop into the tearoom tomorrow when I'm off shift and we can talk then. I'd better get back to it now. Don't fret, love."

"I won't," Flora fibbed, as she hung up and placed the phone back down on the side table. It only now occurred to her that she should perhaps have asked Gregory where her share of the house money was – maybe that was why he was here, to try to get out of paying. Though, it was a very long way to come to convey something that could have easily been passed along through legal channels. Besides, Gregory had never been short of money, so Flora had assumed he was withholding the payment out of spite and not for any other reason.

By this point, she was in no mood to edit her fourth children's story, which sat printed out on the kitchen table, so opted for a bubble bath instead, checking first that the front door was locked and bolted. An unsettled feeling sat in the pit of Flora's stomach, a premonition perhaps of things to come, and she really didn't want to see where it would lead.

THREE

Flora dreamt that she was back in her old house in London, with its three floors and huge reception rooms. Instead of being a comforting reminiscence, it felt foreboding and haunting as Flora seemed to be flying from room to room, able to move through solid objects and wary of any sudden appearances from cupboards or doors. Eventually, she woke feeling disturbed, a sheen of sweat covering her face, and with no chance of getting back to sleep. The clock on her bedside table showed that it was three in the morning, not ideal, but Flora heaved her tired body out of bed and into her fluffy dressing gown. Reggie looked at her inquisitively, his head cocked to one side as if he were assessing whether his own sleep really needed to be disturbed. In the end, he joined Flora as she padded along the tiny corridor to the kitchen.

A cup of chamomile tea made, Flora relaxed back in her favourite armchair beside the log burner which was thankfully still giving out some heat. Her mind drifted between her children's stories of Reggie's escapades, her plans for the tearoom and bookshop and her relationship with Adam. She was determined to keep her thoughts on the positives as the rain lashed the windows and the wind rattled the panes of glass in the old building. Flora hadn't yet got around to having double glazing fitted in the coach house – something which hadn't bothered her in the summer, but which was becoming more of a problem now winter was on the horizon filling her little space with draughts. Thinking that she should, perhaps, have made it a priority rather than focusing so much on the big house and the stable conversion, Flora snuggled down under her warm throw, her eyelids drooping. Reggie was already asleep on the arm of her chair, his little snores and ruffles a comforting background noise. *Perhaps*, Flora told herself just before she drifted off, *I'm getting this all way out of proportion. Perhaps Gregory will be well on his way back down south by now…*

The sky had barely lightened by nine the next morning, so dark were the heavy clouds which covered Baker's Rise. Flora had awoken with a stiff neck and a sore back, her mood matching the miserable weather. Throwing on some old cord leggings and a thick rollneck jumper, she had felt too nauseous to eat any breakfast, so had instead gone straight to the tearoom with Reggie in his carrier. Despite the walk taking no more than five minutes, Flora's thick raincoat was almost soaked through by the time she arrived, and her hair stuck up at odd angles where it had been squashed underneath her knitted bobble hat. Waving briefly at Ted and his builders crew, who seemed to be taking a tea break already, Flora lugged the box of George Jones' finest bakery produce in with her. She immediately felt comforted by the sight of her little tearoom, the six tables arranged around the space, covered with pristine white lace doilies, and just waiting for the beautiful vintage crockery which Flora put out each day. It was cosy, especially with the small table lamps that Flora had added the previous week to ward off the shadows of the encroaching season. They made the place seem cheerier and cast light in all the dark corners.

Flora had been working on her baking skills, and had now almost perfected the scone recipe that Lily had taught her, what seemed like a lifetime ago. Then last month, when they had all begun to recover from the shock of Ray's death and the intrusive police investigation which had followed, she and Lily had again worked together up in the farmhouse kitchen, this time on a fruit pie. That had not been quite as successful, and Flora was still practicing, though her efforts were as yet nowhere near being ready to serve to her customers! She had even tried cheating with pre-made pastry from a supermarket, but the pie had just looked and tasted rather underwhelming – Flora knew she wouldn't want to pay for a slice of it, and certainly didn't expect her customers to.

So, after flicking the switch on the large coffee machine – it was now at least becoming more friend than foe – and running a cleaning cycle for good measure, Flora turned the oven on to preheat while she prepared her scone mixture. With some Classic FM playing in the background, Reggie cooing happily and waddling up and down a separate part of the counter top which Flora had covered with a plastic table cloth for this purpose, and her scones ready to pop in the oven, Flora felt momentarily happy and contented. A far cry from her turmoil of the night before which now seemed, thankfully, just like a bad nightmare. When the bell over the door tinkled, Flora smiled automatically as she looked up from behind the counter, the expression leaving her face just as quickly when she saw who her visitor was.

"Gregory, I thought you would be back in London by now. Surely you need to be at work," it was a statement more than a question, and Flora looked straight back down to her tray of scone dough circles, hoping that if she dismissed the man he might take the hint for once and actually leave.

"I didn't come all of this way, into the back of beyond, to leave without having a proper conversation with you, Flo."

"It's Flora."

"Okay, Flora," Gregory was beginning to look exasperated, his façade of friendship slipping quicker than he would have liked.

Flora felt a sense of pleasure when she saw the man eying Reggie warily, apparently choosing to take no more than three steps into the room towards them.

Reggie, too, seemed annoyed at the intrusion, and squawked, "Not that jerk!" three times in quick succession. Seemingly startled by the parrot's very vocal vehemence, Gregory took a couple of small steps backwards, until he was almost at the door again.

"Good boy, Reggie," Flora said, making it clear whose side she was on in the small confrontation!

"Where did you get that awful bird?" Gregory asked, pulling an immaculately-folded white handkerchief from his pocket and using it to mop his brow.

"Stupid git!" Reggie followed up his previous outburst when he sensed he was being spoken about injuriously!

"Now, Reggie, that is rude," Flora admonished him, though there was little conviction behind her words, "Gregory, Reggie is my best feathered friend. I inherited him."

"Oh? With the estate?" Gregory's ears and eyes pricked up at this and Flora wished she hadn't mentioned her inheritance. It was too late now though, as Gregory took a seat at the table closest to the door.

"I won't bring you a menu as you won't be staying," Flora said tersely, "say what you need to and go."

"Won't you come and sit with me?" Gregory asked, in a little-boy-lost tone that Flora remembered he saved for times when he wanted to butter her up. It wouldn't work today though, nor any day going forward.

"I need to get these in the oven," Flora replied, turning her back on the man and fussing with the tray of unbaked scones. She took much longer than was necessary for the task, disappointed when she didn't hear the tinkle of the bell announcing her unwanted visitor had left. *Did I really expect him to just up and go?* she mused. In the end, there was nothing for it but to hear Gregory out.

"Okay, say it and go," Flora repeated as she strode towards her ex-husband with a confidence she did not feel. Refusing to sit, she stood opposite him with her arms folded across her chest. Reggie had flown to her shoulder, and now he and Flora stared at the intruder with a piercing glare.

"Will you not sit?" Gregory asked again, though with much more irritation in his voice now. Flora smiled inwardly, glad that she was ruffling his feathers.

"We're going round in circles, Gregory, perhaps you should leave," Flora tried to force him out of the door with the power of her will alone, though it proved completely ineffective.

"I want you back Flora," it was said so bluntly, and without any lead-up, that Flora took a step backward.

Reggie, sensing her increased stress and tension, flew to sit on the table in front of Gregory, shrieking, "The fool! The fool!"

When Gregory made a move to swipe the little bird away, Flora pulled herself from her shocked internal dialogue and said in her sternest voice, "Touch him and I won't listen to another single word."

"Very well," Gregory sighed, pulling his arm back whilst eying Reggie with an undisguised, wary distaste, "I've come to get you back, Flora, we've started out on the wrong foot, can we just rewind this whole conversation?"

FOUR

Flora wasn't sure what to say. The short answer was 'no,' the long answer was to list all of the things, over many years, which had led them to getting divorced in the first place. In the end, she chose a shaky middle ground.

"Gregory, we aren't good for each other, you and I. We have always brought out the worst in one another and had we not both been so focused on our careers, we would have split up long before we did. Whatever you think you want, I can assure you it's not me. It wasn't even me you wanted when we were married – your many dalliances proved that!"

"Flora, really, just take a moment…"

Flora held up her finger to quieten him, "I could take

all the moments in the world, Gregory, but it would not persuade me to spend even one more hour trapped in a relationship with you."

"Well, I must say, I expected you to be a bit more… a bit…"

"A bit what? Amenable? Agreeable? I don't know what would have given you that notion. You're not a stupid man – though you are acting it now – so why you think I would welcome your advances… I mean, the divorce wasn't even amicable! You fought me for every penny I was due and you still haven't paid the money I'm owed from you buying me out of the townhouse!"

"You got more than you deserved, and you know it," Gregory bit out. This was the real him showing up now, and Flora was almost glad of it. She couldn't be doing with that silly fake friendship he had affected since his arrival.

"And there we have it. Welcome back the real Gregory!" Flora knew she was riling him up even further.

"Why you! I…" Gregory stood abruptly, scraping his chair back across the wood floor.

"Is this man bothering you?" The bell tinkled at the

same time as Adam rushed in. Flora hadn't heard his car over the sound of the rain against the windows and the blood rushing in her ears from the confrontation. Whilst a part of her did dislike being constantly rescued, as it were, Flora had to admit that she was relieved to have Adam there.

"Who's this?" Gregory asked, staring at Flora with an ugly look in his eyes, "Ah, no, don't tell me, you've got yourself a fancy piece, a dirty little bit on the side…"

"Well! You should talk!" Flora began, as Adam escorted Gregory from the shop, swiftly and none too gently.

The man himself was railing against Flora, casting all kinds of aspersions, until Adam shut the door on him and leant back against it to prevent Gregory coming back in.

"Oh..," it came out as a long moan, and Flora's legs suddenly felt like jelly. She moved into Adam's offered embrace and wrapped her arms tightly around his waist.

"I've got you," he whispered against her hair, "I take it that was him?"

Flora nodded, but couldn't bring herself to look up.

She felt ashamed, possibly because of what Gregory had shouted about her as he was leaving, possibly because her life had yet again started to unravel. She tried to surreptitiously wipe a tear from her eye, feeling Reggie swoop onto her shoulder and nuzzle into her neck.

"What's this?" Adam asked, hooking a finger under Flora's chin to angle her face up to his, "I hope you're not shedding a tear over that pathetic specimen of manhood?" he said gently, bending to place a sweet peck on Flora's forehead.

"No," she whispered, "not him. Just the feelings he evokes. It sends me right back and I feel pathetic for letting him get to me."

"Aw, love, he's really not worth it, and you have a new life now. I'll speak to Pat Hughes and make sure he keeps an eye out for him in the village. If he sees the man, he can warn him off."

"Do you think he'll come back?" Flora hated the tremor in her voice.

"In all honesty? Yes, probably. If he's as tenacious as you say, and there's something that he wants. Yes. That doesn't mean you have to give anything to him, though. Just call me or Pat as soon as he appears, okay?"

It wasn't really okay, not at all, but Flora nodded and squeezed him tighter. This was the last thing she needed in her life right now, but, as usual, she had very little say in the matter.

Unfortunately, the scones were barely salvageable when Flora remembered to rescue them from the oven. They had completely slipped her mind, once it started over-analysing everything that had been said during Gregory's visit. It was Adam who smelled the burning first, and even then it took Flora a moment to remember where the smell could be coming from. Adam stayed for a couple of hours as he was off duty, even helping Flora serve some old ladies from the village and engaging in some flirty banter with them. Flora smiled at his antics, and was grateful that he had stayed to distract her from earlier events.

"So, Fine Flora," he joked when the group had left.

"Just Flora is fine," Flora parried back.

"Okay, Just Flora, how about Sunday lunch in Morpeth with me? Roast dinner and all the trimmings!"

"How could I refuse a meaty offer like that?" Flora

continued with their light flirting, wondering how she would keep herself distracted when he was gone.

"Excellent, shall I pick you up or do you want to just drive across?"

"It's silly you coming all the way over here, just to drive straight back! I'll make my own way and meet you at the restaurant."

"Perfect," Adam leaned down to kiss her, more intensely this time, and Flora melted into him.

"Yuck!" came the squawk from across the room, and they both laughed as they pulled away.

"Hey cheeky! You're cramping my style!" Adam replied, as Reggie puffed out his feathers and jutted out his little chest.

"Don't worry, I'll leave him at home on Sunday," Flora laughed, happy to hear the tinkle of the doorbell as Adam was gathering his things to leave.

"Tanya!" Flora couldn't have been happier to see her friend.

Spying Flora and Adam alone, Tanya asked, "Shall I come back? It's nothing urgent!"

"Not at all, I'm actually just leaving," Adam reassured

her, before giving Flora one last peck on the cheek and taking his leave.

"Such a sweet couple," Tanya said, winking at Flora before plopping herself down at the table nearest the counter.

Flora felt herself blush as she took the seat next to her friend.

"She's a corker!" Reggie chimed into the conversation.

"So, what can I do for you?" Flora asked, smiling.

"Ah, well I think it is more what I can do for you!" Tanya replied cryptically, "I have seen Betty this morning at Jean's shop and she is worried about you. Says you are spreading yourself too flatly or something. Anyway, I got the gist. She thinks you do too much."

"Ah, I can imagine she had a few words to say on that subject, yes," Flora nodded, "so, what is your idea?"

"Well, in Ukraine I was actress – just amateur you understand, nothing serious."

"You are certainly a lady of many surprises! And talents!" Flora laughed.

"Yes, so I thought maybe you would like some help

with the talent show? Auditions and rehearsals? We really should be getting started..."

Flora jumped up and gave Tanya a big hug, "Thank you! Yes, that would be perfect – I have a suggestion for you too!"

"Oh?"

"In the new year, when the bookshop is open, I'll be needing to take on another member of staff for the tearoom and..."

"Yes! I will do it! Thank you!" Now they were both laughing and hugging each other, until Flora pulled away to make them a celebratory pot of tea.

Funnily enough, Tanya was exactly the person that Flora needed to confide in about Gregory. She had had enough problems of her own with her ex, Dmitriy, in the past, and so was able to empathise with Flora's fears. It felt good for Flora to spill her worries to someone unconnected to her romantic entanglements, and Tanya was reassuring in her advice.

"Yes, I understand about men who are like dog with a bone, believe me, that is why I had to take drastic action and run away from my relationship. He made me isolated there, I had no friends to turn to. You, though, you have me, Betty and Harry, Shona, and Adam of course. You have support here, he cannot get to you."

"Thank you, Tanya, yes, I hadn't thought of it like that."

"And you can call my Pat, any time, and he will come help you," Tanya added, somewhat proudly.

"Of course, I will do," Flora felt the ball of anxiety in her stomach melt slightly. After all, what could Gregory do if she steadfastly refused to listen to his demands? Very little other than to go back to London with his tail between his legs. Or so Flora hoped.

FIVE

When the weekend dawned the next day, the rain hadn't abated and there were an increasing number of stories on the local news about flooding and crashes caused by the slippery road conditions. Flora planned to work in the tearoom until three and then close up and pop to Betty's to make the much-anticipated Christmas cake. Apparently, it had to mature for several weeks after baking, and Flora was to be in charge of it whilst Betty went on her cruise. Although Flora was excited to make the rich fruit cake, and to learn a recipe that she could hopefully use for years to come, she did feel slightly under pressure to not do anything to damage the delicacy whilst it was in her care! Betty had been very particular in her request that Flora was to 'feed' the cake until two weeks before Christmas, when she was to leave it for a week to dry out and then they would work together again to cover it in fondant icing and festive decorations. Flora had no idea what it meant to 'feed' a cake, so she hoped this afternoon's lesson would prove enlightening! What's more, the thought of icing it filled her with dread, but *one thing at a time* Flora told herself, as was her new motto.

Reggie was clearly rather disgruntled to be deposited back home on Saturday afternoon, despite him having spent an enjoyable morning in the tearoom playing with the Marshall girls, who had made the rather soggy trek up from the village with their mum, Sally. The Vicar wasn't with them on this occasion, so the girls vied for their mum's attention, and took turns moving between Sally's lap and Flora's. It pleased Flora, though, and for the first time in a long while she felt a small regret for things that might have been. She had always wanted her own family, but when it hadn't happened naturally or through IVF, Gregory had been flat against them trying any other route such as adoption. When she thought of it now, the way he had taken something so fundamental as being a mother away from her, it made Flora angry. She blinked away a tear and focussed on little Megan on her lap, wriggly as always, and shovelling big chunks of chocolate cake into her mouth whilst listening to her mum talk about the new knitting and crochet club she wanted to start in the village.

"It could be called Knit and Natter," Sally had said excitedly, looking to Flora for approval.

"What? No charming rhyming title?" Flora joked, referring to all the names which rhymed with Baker's Rise, "How about Baker's Rise Hooks and Eyes?"

"Oh, now that is good!" Sally laughed along with her, "I'll bear it in mind! I thought to have it in the church hall at first, but then I was wondering, when your cosy book nook is open, if we might..?"

"Meet there? Oh yes, that's a perfect idea!" Flora agreed, feeling a frisson of excitement at the thought that her new little venture could become a hub for village social life, limited as it was!

"Excellent, thank you Flora!"

"Are you an expert knitter yourself?" Flora had asked, genuinely interested.

"No, hardly proficient at all really," Sally laughed, "What with the girls to look after and my duties as vicar's wife, I just really do it in the evenings for a bit of relaxation. It's Jean from the shop who'll be leading the group, giving us all some tips and tricks. Will you be joining us?"

Absence Makes the Heart Grow Fondant

"I will certainly try," Flora had replied, thinking she could do with a calming activity right now, as it happened.

So, after the family had left and Flora had cleared everything up, she dropped Reggie at the coach house and made her way to Betty's, battling through the wind and rain. It was pointless even trying to use her umbrella, as it kept turning inside out, so Flora held onto her woollen hat and rushed on, arriving at Betty's tiny cottage soaked and out of breath.

"Get yerself in lass," Betty said, flinging the door open before Flora had even reached the doorstep, having been watching for her through the window, "it's pitchin' for a storm tonight, to be sure!"

"I think you might be right there, Betty," Flora replied, forcing the door closed behind her against the gusts of wind which were trying to keep it open.

"I've made us a pot of tea, and set out all the ingredients, but you'll have to do the mixing as this wet weather is making my old hip ache something rotten."

"Oh no, the one they just put in?"

"No lass, the old one. The new one is fit as a fiddle, I just have to be careful not to do too much while I'm in the last stages of it healing. I want to be feeling my best when we set off on our Caribbean adventure on Monday!"

"Oh, well, okay, as long as you give me all the directions," Flora said hesitantly, feeling the cake-making pressure firmly on her shoulders now.

"And of course, you'll be privy to Granny Lafferty's special ingredient, so you must promise to take the recipe to the grave, or at least keep quiet till I'm dead and buried," Betty said, rather sombrely.

Flora had the inappropriate urge to giggle, "Well, that does seem rather morbid, Betty, but yes, I agree!" Flora pressed two fingers against her lips and then to her heart as a sign of silent promise as the two women made their way into the kitchen, now that Flora was divested of her wet coat, hat and boots. Little Tina lay on her dog bed by the fire, merely opening sleepy eyes to see who had disturbed her cosy slumber and giving out a tiny bark for effect.

Betty sat at the tiny kitchen table, her bright eyes watching keenly to ensure Flora followed her instructions to the letter, whilst Flora stood at the small electric hob, stirring a pan with the first of the ingredients in it – the dried fruit, orange and lemon zests, softened butter and soft brown sugar.

"And so, now for the secret," Betty announced when the ingredients had begun to blend, "Granny Lafferty didn't do things by halves, so now we add the alcohol to the pan – brandy in this case – but Granny insisted we always add double of any alcohol in the recipe. Both at this stage and for feeding the cake!"

"Double!" Flora asked, incredulous, the urge to giggle strong again.

"Aye lass, double. She said it added to the flavour."

"Was Granny Lafferty fond of a tipple at other times?" Flora asked, trying to keep a straight face.

"Funny you should mention that lass, she was a bit partial to the odd dram, yes," Betty blushed, making Flora wonder if she was recalling some alcohol-fuelled antics of Granny Lafferty's!

Once this stage was completed, Flora carefully tipped the mixture into a large bowl, adding the other ingredients such as the flour, eggs and spices. Betty watched her reverently, as if this was a sacred annual ritual, which must be followed action by action without error. Stirring the bowl, Flora felt beads of sweat rise on her forehead – not from exertion, rather from the pressure of being under Betty's scrutiny for so long. The task complete, with a lesson in how to stir correctly thrown in for good measure, Betty showed Flora how to line the cake tin with a double layer of baking parchment and then to wrap a double layer of newspaper around the outside of the tin, tying with string to secure it.

With the cake finally in the oven, Betty returned to her normal, jovial self, and Flora breathed a sigh of relief, making a fresh pot of tea for them and sitting down for a quick chat. The sky had darkened to near black outside, and Flora knew she mustn't leave it too long before once again fighting the elements on her walk back to the coach house.

SIX

Flora finally rounded the small path which led to the coach house, her hat dripping fat droplets down her face, her legs so wet that her trousers were plastered to her legs uncomfortably, and her rubber wellington boots filled with a layer of water in which Flora's feet squelched around uncomfortably. She had her head down to brace against the wind, so did not see the car sitting in front of her house until she was almost upon it.

"Gregory!" Flora exclaimed to the man getting out of the driver's side, "What on earth are you doing back here?" The anger in her tone was evident, and Flora stormed past her ex-husband and up to her front door, keen to get inside and out of the persistent wind and rain.

It was as Gregory made to be following right on Flora's

heels into the house that she spun around just inside the door and yelled above the weather, "What are you doing?"

"Oh, come on Flora! You can't expect me to stand outside in this!"

"I didn't expect you to be here at all!" Flora's temper was thoroughly frayed now, and she stood, dripping, with her hands on her hips, adamant that she would not budge and let him in.

"Please, Flora, I just want to talk to you."

The sound of flapping wings came up the hallway behind her, and Flora heard Reggie before she saw him, "Not that jerk!" he shrieked, before going straight over Flora and hovering above Gregory, underneath the shelter of the umbrella. Then Reggie did something that Flora had never seen him do before – he dropped a rather unpleasant package right on Gregory's head, on the bald patch which he always tried to keep covered, but which had been exposed by the wind.

"Argh," Gregory shouted, reaching his hand up to the rather disgusting substance which now coated his scalp, "that wretched bird, I'll wring its neck!" He lunged ineffectually upwards, but Reggie was already behind Flora, sitting on the hallway radiator and looking rather pleased with himself. Flora didn't have the heart to scold him, but nor did she feel like giggling as she normally would at the sight of her prim and proper ex-husband with bird poo running down his forehead.

At that moment, the headlights from another vehicle came up the small driveway, and Flora prayed that it would be Adam. As much as she hated this – apparently all-too regular – need to be rescued, she had to admit that she would be glad of it right now, especially since Gregory looked as if he were about to explode. No such luck. Whilst Flora did recognise the car, it did not belong to her Detective Bramble. No, the car in view was owned by none other than Phil Drayford. *Great*, Flora thought, *that's just what I need.*

Oblivious to the new visitor, who was currently parking behind his own vehicle, Greg ploughed on regardless, his lips pursed in a tight grimace, no doubt from trying to keep a check on his anger, "I think we still have a chance, Flora, at a future… together."

"You must be suffering from some kind of amnesia, Gregory," Flora shouted, "how could you have forgotten how things really were between us? It wasn't a marriage. It was a business partnership – and a bad one at that. One we should have dissolved many years ago! We haven't even been in touch for months, except via our solicitors, how did you even know how to find me?"

"I saw you in a news article online – at that village fete."

Flora's heart sank at the thought he'd seen that embarrassing interview, but she stood her ground, "Well, it makes no difference. Your journey has been wasted!"

"Fine!" Gregory's face revealed his true anger now, the veins in his temple twitching rapidly and his bulging eyes blazing, "Fine, well, I will be making my claim for half of this estate via my solicitor in London. I'm sure I should be owed it since you'd moved up here before the divorce!"

Flora stood, stunned into silence. Having rushed from his car to stay as dry as possible, Phil hovered now just behind Gregory, apparently seeking shelter under the man's ridiculously huge umbrella, so he must have heard every word. Sensing his presence, Gregory turned and asked, "Who the hell are you?"

"Never mind who he is," Flora yelled, all sense of propriety gone now, she just needed Gregory to leave and to get rid of Phil too. *Of all the people to witness this!*

"You can waste your money on the legal route if you like, but you can rest assured the result will be the same – you see, I had a feeling you would come back at some point, shuffling in with your tail between your legs and making demands, so I made sure to not sign the final papers accepting the inheritance until after our divorce was all finalised!"

"You cow!" Gregory raised his arm, but it was caught mid-air by Phil, who used it to swing the man around to face him.

"And that's your cue to leave," Phil said, the tone in his voice brooking no argument.

Gregory took one final look at Flora, spat on the ground at her feet and snarled, "This won't be the last you hear of this!" before he wrenched his arm from Phil's grasp and made his way back to his car, the umbrella almost pulling him off his feet as it caught in the increasingly-urgent gusts of wind.

"I'm sorry you had to see that," Flora said, to the sound of Gregory's screeching tyres as he tried to manoeuvre his car around Phil's.

"I'd better go and back up to let him out, or he'll barge mine out of the way," Phil said, though he did not move from the spot, as if waiting to see if he should come back afterwards.

"Yes, then I suppose you'd better come in," Flora felt she couldn't send the man on his way without giving him the chance to speak his piece – not after how he'd just stepped in on her behalf. But the thought of owing Phil any kind of debt – even one of gratitude – did not sit easily with her.

"Reginald Parrot," Flora said to the bird on her arm, once she and Phil were inside, with the front door closed behind them, and the kettle on, "Reginald Parrot, that was a bad bird! Bad bird! We don't do that to people!"

"My Flora!" he squawked defiantly, "she's a corker!"

Of course, Flora couldn't help but be buttered up by his cheeky playfulness, until, that is, Reggie took off from her arm, swooped at Phil and screeched, "the fool has arrived" twice in quick succession.

"Cage now!" Flora said firmly, not wanting to deal with another angry man so soon after the last.

"So," Flora said, when they were both in the sitting room with a cup of Earl Grey, "what can I do for you, Phil?"

"Nothing actually," Phil said, "I just wanted to let you know that I spoke to Shona about the whole paternity thing…"

"Really?" Flora interrupted, thinking that was probably the last thing the young woman needed while she still grieved her father. She knew that Phil had been plagued by questions after Harold had tried to blackmail him with assertions the man who he believed to be his dad wasn't in fact his biological father – especially after seeing two of Ray's estranged sons at the village fete and recognising an undeniable similarity in appearance – but to take it up with Shona so soon was a bit much.

"Yes, I, ah, waited until a decent length of time had passed after the funeral of course," Phil rushed on, "and she agreed to do a paternity test with her DNA and mine and, well, it was a match for the same paternity. Ray Dodds was my father, which makes Shona my half-sister. I will never know now if the man himself ever knew the truth."

Flora was unsure how to react, since she didn't know how Phil would deal with this, having believed for most of his life that Alf Drayford was his father. So she simply nodded and waited.

"Of course," Phil went on, "I'd like to build a

relationship with Shona, eventually, given I have no siblings myself. But all in good time. What I really came here for was to apologise for putting pressure on you about getting access to Harold's files."

"Oh, well, thank you, Phil," Flora was definitely ready for this strange conversation to be over. It was true, that in a village this size everyone knew each other's business – even if you hadn't asked for the information. Flora had enough on her mind right now, wondering what Gregory's next move would be, without thinking too much about Phil's familial situation.

"I was hoping, Flora, that we could move past all of the… the awkwardness of the past couple of months, and be friends again? I hear you're making a bookshop, I would love to help with that in any way I can."

"That's very kind," Flora struggled to keep up a positive demeanour, when she wasn't sure how she felt about having any kind of relationship with the man again, "I'll let you know if I need anything once the stable conversion is finished."

"Very well," Phil smiled and, to Flora's relief, stood up to leave, "I'd best be getting back before the full force of the storm hits."

Flora's head whirred with the events of the past hour as she saw Phil out. His visit had been harmless, an olive branch, even, but Flora had no headspace for it right now. No, now she needed to think what to do about Gregory, for surely he was a threat she couldn't ignore.

SEVEN

Lying in bed that night, unable to sleep whilst she listened to the rain lashing the windows, and the wind howling around the small building, Flora contemplated Gregory's words once again. She had not been lying when she'd told him that he had no claim to the Baker's Rise estate, of that she was certain – especially as Harry Bentley had confirmed the fact – so on that front Flora had no worries. Gregory was a man who would not take no for an answer, however, and Flora had grave concerns about what his next move would be. That he was, for some reason, in dire need of money, was clear, but to what lengths would he go to get it? She was also now regretting the fact that she had called neither Pat Hughes nor Adam to tell them that her ex-husband had turned up once again. Whether it was embarrassment, hurt pride, or a mixture of both,

Flora was now re-thinking her stubborn desire to deal with everything herself. Perhaps having the police speak to the man was not such a bad idea, and Flora resolved to talk to Adam about her latest encounter when she saw him for lunch the next day. Hopefully, he would have some professional advice on how to deal with tenacious ex-husbands, even though he was probably too close to Flora to think objectively.

Sunday came around all too quickly for Flora, who had finally managed to drop off to sleep at four in the morning. This meant she slept late, missed church and then rushed to get ready for her midday date in Morpeth. The storm seemed to have abated somewhat, with only the rain left to deal with, so Flora opted for a woollen knee-length dress in navy and heeled, tan leather boots which also reached the knee. Accessorizing the outfit with the beautiful amethyst necklace which Adam had bought her for Betty and Harry's wedding, Flora felt well put-together. Her hair was still in the neat bob which Amy had created – albeit slightly longer – and Flora tied a silk scarf round her head to protect the style until she reached the restaurant. Sadly, her raincoat was still wet from the previous day, so Flora chose an open-fronted wool coat, which was waist length and fastened with only a belt. Figuring she would only be in the car and then the restaurant, Flora thought it would suffice if she also used her umbrella.

Saying a quick goodbye to Reggie, who had watched all of her primping and preening with a look of disdain, Flora rushed out of the coach house and along to the tearoom, where she had left her car parked. Bits of broken branches and twigs littered the small pathway, and Flora was relieved to find the tearoom still in one piece with no apparent damage to its roof or windows. After a quick check of the building behind, to make sure the builders had left it locked up and safe from the weather, Flora rushed to her car to begin the drive to Morpeth. Before reaching the main road to the large town, Flora first had to navigate the country roads which led out of the village and through Baker's Bottom – an area at the foot of the hill, which was mostly forest, but for a couple of small farms – known affectionately by the locals as 'The Rear End.' The road through this rather unfortunately-named space of a few square miles, twisted and turned, with sharp corners and blind summits. Flora knew better than to rush, especially in this weather, so she took the drive slowly having allowed herself enough time to do it comfortably.

It was when Flora was almost through this area of countryside, and nearly at the main road, that she spotted what looked to be a parked car off the road up ahead. On closer inspection, over to the left and a short way into the sparse woodland, it appeared that the front of the silver saloon was smashed up against the trunk of a tree. Worse than that, though, Flora thought she recognised the vehicle. Pulling up on the side of the road, Flora slipped and tripped her way across the narrow grass verge and into the woodland, where the thick carpet of rotting leaves and broken branches was now a rather squelchy, wet layer of mud. With every step Flora took, her heels were sucked deeper into the dense mulch, until she finally reached her destination. Flora held her breath for fear of what she would find. Both the driver's side and the passenger door were open, but there was no sign of anyone inside the car. Flora wasn't sure whether this was a good thing or not, as she leaned into the vehicle and peered around the interior which was soaking from the rain. Save for a few patches of what appeared to be blood on the passenger seat – which caused Flora to shudder more than the freezing cold rain which was pelting her – all looked normal. Reluctantly, Flora did a circuit of the outside, as much as she was able around the tree, looking for she didn't know what – a body? Flora prayed not. As much as she disliked Gregory, she had no desire to find him dead. When that search, too, came up empty, Flora hurried as fast as her squelching boots would allow her back to her own car, finally releasing a long breath when she was safely back inside.

Flora's heart beat with rhythmic fury and her hands shook with anxiety as she dialled Adam's number and waited to hear his reassuring voice on the other end of the line.

"Slow down, love," he said, when she had gabbled her way through an explanation, "You say he's been rear-ended?"

"No, his car is in The Rear End – I mean, in Baker's Bottom, you know that wooded area just outside the village?"

"Oh, well, what's it doing there? And why are you with it?"

"I found it!" Flora shrieked, getting exasperated now at having to explain herself twice, "When I was driving to meet you."

"And it's crashed you say?"

"Yes, into a tree!"

"So, is he okay, your ex? Have you called an ambulance?"

"No, I can't find him!" Flora felt the tears threatening to fall and struggled to hold herself together.

"Okay, love, text me the co-ordinates from your satnav and I'll be there as soon as possible. About half an hour."

"I'm sorry about lunch," Flora was sobbing now, but Adam had already hung up.

The wait for Adam to arrive seemed to take forever, and Flora shivered in her car despite having the heating on full blast. It did cross her mind that she should have called Pat Hughes, he being much closer, but Flora had been too panicked to think straight, and in any case he was likely in church. Finally, headlights from the opposite direction brought a glimmer of hope, which did indeed turn out to be Adam.

"So," Adam said pulling Flora into a hug as she got out of the car and ran to meet him as he pulled up in front of her, "I have to admit to being a bit confused, love, do you want to show me the car?"

Flora took Adam down to the abandoned vehicle, grateful of his steady arm to hold her up through another trek in the mud. Adam's face was grave as he took a cursory glance around the inside of the car, then left Flora holding onto the tree as he walked the same circuit she had earlier. Their mixed footprints were now littering the area, and Adam seemed annoyed that they were obscuring any other footprints that may have been there.

"I'll have to radio this in," he said eventually, "and I'm afraid there'll be some questions for you to answer, I should think."

"For me?" Flora squawked, in a good impersonation of Reggie.

"Yes, love," Adam's brows were pinched together and he looked concerned.

"Just about how I found the car, you mean?"

"Well, that and when you last saw the man, that kind of thing. You haven't seen him since I escorted him from the tearoom have you?"

"Well, actually…"

"Oh Flora," Adam scraped his hands through his wet hair.

"Actually, he came round yesterday evening," Flora told Adam what had happened.

"Did anyone witness this?"

"Yes, Phil Drayford," Flora's stomach sank as she thought how Phil had heard their raised voices.

"Oh my word, Flora, you do get yourself in these scrapes, don't you! Why on earth did you not call me straight away last night?" Adam seemed angry now, though Flora knew it was just from worry about her.

She didn't reply, simply swallowed down the lump in her throat and tried not to cry again as Adam made the necessary calls. His expression and tone of voice, coupled with the side of the conversation which Flora could hear, told her things did not bode well for a swift resolution. Not at all.

EIGHT

The police headquarters in Morpeth was as grim as Flora remembered – worse even in the dark gloom of the November day. Bramble had been told in no uncertain terms that he was too close to the case to be allowed to investigate it, so now Flora sat facing Blackett, and a female detective whose name she had been told was McArthur. Having been whisked away in Blackett's car, whilst a team of officers searched the crash site, it had been all Flora could do to retain her composure. Adam had followed behind in his own vehicle, but Flora had not seen him since entering the police station. Thankfully, she was only here voluntarily, to 'help the officers with their enquiries,' so Flora didn't have to go through any kind of booking in process.

She sat now, in an interview room very similar to the

one in which she had first spoken to Bramble. That felt like a very long time ago, but could only be less than four short months. The room was empty, save for the chairs and table at which the three of them now sat. Nor did it have any window to shed any light on proceedings, and a simple, unadorned lightbulb swung above them. A musty smell pervaded Flora's senses, and for a moment she wondered when the room had last been cleaned and who had sat in the chair before her. Germs were the least of her problems, however.

Blackett went through the basics of her name and address, advising Flora that the interview would be recorded, before he jumped into the crux of the matter.

"So, Mrs. Miller, please can you explain your relationship to the owner of the crashed vehicle."

"Yes, it belongs to my ex-husband, Gregory Temple."

"You do not share a surname?"

"I reverted to my maiden name during the separation and we are now fully divorced."

"I see," Blackett shuffled his papers on the table with his thin, bony fingers, though his eyes never once left Flora's face, "And do you have any idea where Mr. Temple is now?"

"I do not," Flora tried hard to not let her voice waver, but she feared her emotions betrayed her.

"And when did you last see him."

"Yesterday evening, at my home in Baker's Rise."

"Was he there by invitation?"

"I, ah…"

"Were you expecting him, Mrs. Miller?"

"Ah, no."

"And what was the nature of his visit?"

"Ostensibly, to tell me that he wanted me back. Which he didn't really, you see, he just wanted a share of Baker's Estate," Flora realised she was wringing her hands painfully on her lap and tried to stop herself.

"I understand that you inherited the property earlier this year?"

"Yes, that is correct. After my divorce."

"I see. So, am I to understand that Mr. Temple had had a wasted journey?"

"Yes."

"And how did he react to that?"

"Ah, well, badly," Flora whispered.

"Did anyone witness your... discussion?"

"Yes, Phil Drayford from the village, but he is..."

"Just answer the questions, please, Mrs. Miller," Blackett's tone brooked no argument, "and then Mr. Temple left? In the car which is now crashed at Baker's Bottom?"

"Yes."

"Are you sure you haven't seen him since he departed your property, Mrs. Miller?" Blackett implied he didn't believe her, and Flora wondered why the other detective stayed so silent.

"I am positive, yes," Flora tried to sound firm, but her traitorous voice wobbled.

"And you have no idea where Mr. Temple is now?"

"None."

"Were you aware that there is a substance resembling blood on the passenger seat of his vehicle?"

"Pardon?" Flora was confused by the sudden shift in direction, "Well, I did notice some red, yes, though I only had a cursory glance inside."

"A cursory glance, you say? I'd be interested, then, to know how this necklace came to be in the footwell of the car. Is it yours?" Blackett produced Flora's amethyst necklace, causing her to breathe in sharply.

Flora tried to feel her neck inconspicuously, though Blackett's beady eyes were still watching her every move. Her collar bone felt worryingly bare, "Yes, it looks like the one I was wearing today. It must've fallen off when I…"

"When you were what, Mrs. Miller? Sitting in the vehicle with your ex-husband?"

"What? No! I…"

"Did you cause him to veer off the road and crash, Mrs. Miller?"

"No! I've told you, I wasn't there when the car crashed!"

"Hmm," Blackett couldn't have looked less believing of her story.

But then, Flora thought to herself, *what else did I expect from the man? Adam has told me in the past that his colleague disapproves of our relationship – not least because*

I keep being embroiled in murder cases!

"So, Mrs. Miller," Detective McArthur finally spoke up. A broad woman, with a round face that managed to look both chubby and angular, her stare was no less piercing than Blackett's. Certainly, no smile or other reassuring expression was forthcoming, "to summarise, you were potentially the last to see your ex-husband before his apparent disappearance – whether that was yesterday evening as you say or much more recently is yet to be confirmed. There was no love lost between you. There is blood to evidence a potential crime, and your necklace was found embedded inside his vehicle, your footprints surrounding it, and you were conveniently the one to find it. Out of everyone in the area, it was you. Correct?"

"Well, when you put it like that, I…"

"Correct?"

"Yes," Flora whispered.

"Very well," Blackett spoke up again now, "Please do not leave the village, Mrs. Miller, as I'm sure we will be requiring you to help us with our enquiries again very soon."

"Am I to be charged?" Flora forced herself to voice her greatest fear.

"We do not know the exact nature of the crime, as yet," McArthur said, avoiding a direct answer.

"Very well, you are free to leave," Blackett finally took his gaze from Flora's face, effectively dismissing her.

McArthur stood and indicated for Flora to follow her out, which Flora did, her legs unsteady and her mind whirring.

"I will have an officer drive you back to your car," McArthur said tersely.

"Oh, I think Detective Bramble might..." Flora began.

"Detective Bramble has been instructed by our superiors to cease all contact with you for the duration of the case," McArthur interrupted.

Flora felt the tears spring to her eyes and tried hard to swallow down the lump in her throat. She was determined not to let this woman see her cry, as she was directed outside to a squad car where a tall, lanky police officer was waiting.

"We will be in touch, Mrs. Miller. Thank you for helping us with our investigation," and with that,

McArthur turned and left Flora in the doorway, her eyes blurred from tears and her whole body shaking with the effort of holding them in.

NINE

When Flora was unceremoniously left by the side of the road, she let herself into her own car and sat there for several long minutes, allowing the tears to finally fall. Over to her left, the area had been cordoned off and numerous people were at work, combing the forest, presumably for clues as to Gregory's whereabouts. In the distance, Flora thought she spotted Pat Hughes and his police dog, Frank, searching the woodland which became denser the farther you walked into it. Unable to bear the scene any longer, Flora did a U-turn on the quiet road and headed back up the hill to Baker's Rise, driving slowly as befitted her nervy state. She saw Shona as she drove along Front Street, and Flora gave a quick wave in response to Shona's own greeting, but couldn't bring herself to pull over for a chat. It was well past lunchtime now, and her stomach was grumbling the lack of food, even though Flora herself felt like she had no appetite at all. In fact, her main feeling was one of nausea.

The journey, which in reality was only five minutes, seemed to take an age, and Flora was relieved to finally make her way up the short driveway to the coach house. The moment she turned in, and saw Adam's car waiting, Flora burst into a renewed bout of tears. Just to see him there, his familiar form getting out of his car into the heavy drizzle, made her desperate for a hug and his warm reassurance.

"Adam! I didn't expect to see you, but I'm so thankful that you're here," Flora left her own car and rushed towards him, as Adam hurried to her, the pair meeting in the middle, "Detective McArthur said you couldn't…"

"Aye, I know, the Detective Chief Inspector has banned me from dealing with the investigation, given my close relationship to you, and made it clear that even seeing you would be unwise for my career."

"Oh Adam, then why are you..?"

"Here? Because I love you, and I'm not going to let you go through this alone. I've been married to my career since I joined the force in my early twenties. It's the reason I never settled down with anyone. But I'm not prepared to lose you because of it. Promotion be damned. Now, let's get you inside."

Flora unlocked the door, and the pair were met by a very loud parrot, squawking, "What time do you call this?" and swooping down onto Flora's shoulder, deliberately ignoring the man with her.

"Now, now," Flora tried to cajole the bird, "let's get you some grapes," she hurried into the kitchen and dumped her handbag on the chair, "I'll put the kettle on and we can have tea and cake and..," Flora rushed on to try to tamp down the rising sense of panic which was threatening to engulf her.

"Flora, Flora, love, come here," Adam moved behind her and rubbed his arms from Flora's shoulders down to her wrists, ending with taking hold of her hands. Flora leaned back against him, trying to take deep breaths, before her whole body crumpled, and she sagged forwards, her head in her hands which she pulled away from Adam's, and her torso almost bent double. Adam turned her gently and helped Flora to straighten up into his embrace.

"I've got you, I've got you," he whispered, holding the sobbing Flora to him, as her knees seemed to buckle under the weight of her distress, "let's get you sat down, hey?"

They moved into the sitting room, with Flora leaning heavily on Adam for support, until she was sat in her favourite armchair. Adam pulled the throw from the couch and laid it over her knees, kissed her on the forehead and then moved to light the log burner in the fireplace to give the room some warmth. Reggie, apparently regretting his earlier outburst, came to sit on the arm of Flora's chair, chirping, "My Flora," softly on repeat. When Adam had made them both some sweet tea, Flora moved to join him on the sofa, where she sat with her legs over his lap, the blanket covering them.

"I'm so sorry about that... that, mental breakdown," Flora said, feeling embarrassed.

"Don't be, really," Adam whispered, "you have every right to be upset," he put down his mug of tea on the side table and shuffled closer so that he could hold both of Flora's hands. He brought them to his mouth and gently kissed her palms before saying, "we're in this together. I don't care what the protocol is for me being so close to you. As far as I'm concerned, as long as I'm not involved in the case, then there's no conflict of interest – you're my top priority, Flora."

"Thank you," Flora whispered, turning sideways and laying her head on Adam's shoulder. He bent down and kissed her head then put his arm around her shoulders, hugging her close.

"So, love, as painful as it is, how about you tell me the whole story, from the beginning, and we'll see what we can figure out. I might be able to get some information from McArthur, we have a good working relationship but I don't want to push it and raise any suspicion."

Flora recounted each of Gregory's visits in detail, expanding on exactly what was said, and ending with Phil's arrival and her ex-husband's angry exit. The more she recalled each conversation, the angrier she became, which was a much better feeling that the helplessness Flora had been experiencing up to this point.

"So, what will happen now?" she eventually asked, "I don't want to have this hanging over me the way the investigation into Ray's death did. It was like a black cloud over everyone, and I wasn't even directly implicated in that!"

"Well, as it stands, there is only evidence of a road traffic accident. They'll be trying to locate the man himself, by leaving messages on his mobile phone, by speaking to anyone at his address, getting contact details for business associates and so forth. He could have a concussion and just have wandered off, so of course they'll keep combing the area, bring in the sniffer dogs and all that. There's a long way to go before they could formally accuse you of anything. But," Adam paused, clearly wondering if he should say what he was about to, "but they'll want to talk to you more, love, a lot more, as you're the only tangible lead in the case right now."

"Oh," Flora said, her heart sinking before she pulled herself together again, "well, I suspected as much. Shall I just go on as normal then, or maybe try to investigate myself..?"

"No, please don't get any more involved than you are already. Promise me, love," Adam's eyes were firm and his mouth was set in a hard line.

"Okay, I promise," though Flora wasn't too happy with the idea of stepping back and letting the police do everything.

"I can still help with the decorating in the book shop," Adam was clearly trying to change the subject now, "it turns out taking my leave days this week couldn't have been better timed," he smiled, but it didn't quite reach his eyes.

"Yes, they're knocking through the wall at the back of

the tearoom tomorrow, so I need to go in this evening and make sure everything is moved and covered. I started that on Friday, so there's not too much left to do. Then, when the dust is cleaned up, they will just need to do the last finishing off tasks, but from tomorrow we can start decorating at the other end of the bookshop," Flora tried, but failed, to muster some enthusiasm.

"Okay, so I'll make us some late," he checked his watch, "very late lunch, and then we'll go together to the tearoom and do everything on your list."

"Really? Thank you," Flora kissed him briefly on the lips, before a thought struck her, "Oh my goodness! Betty and Harry are leaving for their cruise in the early hours of tomorrow morning, so I need to go round to say goodbye and collect the Christmas cake!"

"Okay, don't panic, we'll eat, we'll visit, then we'll sort the tearoom!" Adam stood and rearranged the throw over Flora's legs, handing her the remote control for the television, "Watch something to take your mind off things while I cook," he said, heading into the kitchen.

Reggie snuggled into the crook of Flora's neck and chirped quietly. Although seemingly calm on the outside, Flora's head whirred relentlessly with her inner thoughts. She needed to do something to find

Gregory, but what?

TEN

It turned out that Adam made a mean pasta bake, and Flora felt slightly better once she had something on her stomach. The rain had started up again in earnest, and the pair bundled up in their thick coats, opting to drive to Betty's cottage rather than walk down into the village.

"If you don't mind," Flora began, once they were in Adam's car, "I'd rather we don't tell Betty or Harry anything about recent events. Heaven forbid that they decide to stay at home and support me. They really deserve this holiday, and it is their honeymoon after all, so I don't want there to be any chance they'll miss out."

"Of course, I completely agree, we'll just say we decided to have lunch at home instead of in Morpeth, because of the weather."

Absence Makes the Heart Grow Fondant

It was warm and cosy in the older couple's home, though Betty did shed a few tears when she handed little Tina over to Shona for safekeeping while she was away.

"Aw, don't worry, she'll have a fab time with me and Aaron, won't she?" Shona asked her son. Aaron nodded his head excitedly, and the pair left with a huge bag full of Tina's treats and toys, plus two dog beds, a large bag of food, a variety of leads and harnesses, and some little doggy winter coats in various materials and styles.

"I think that dog's packed more than me!" Harry joked as they waved to Shona and Aaron across the street.

"Now about this cake," Betty said, drying her eyes and looking very seriously at Flora, "it has to be fed at least once a week…"

"I thought the recipe said once a fortnight?" Flora asked, slightly confused, and not trusting her own memory any more.

"Aye lass, but remember Granny Lafferty's secret? So, double the measure, twice as often!"

"Oh!" Flora said, wondering if that wouldn't make for a very boozy bake!

"Yes, so, don't you forget, that'll be four times while I'm away, put it in the notebook on your phone or something."

"Yes, Betty," Flora found it was easier just to agree when Betty was on one of her missions!

When Flora and Adam managed to leave, after two cups of tea and two pieces of carrot cake each, Flora felt rather despondent at the thought of not seeing her two friends for a month – a month which she imagined was about to be very trying.

"Chin up," Adam whispered when they got in the car and plastered smiles on their faces, whilst waving to the older couple, "there's everything to look forward to, you know."

Flora nodded, but inside she felt like weeping.

They managed to sort the tearoom in record time, since there were two of them to move the tables and chairs up to the end of the room nearest the counter. Flora had already covered the coffee machine and counter tops in plastic sheeting, so all that remained was to cover the stacked tables and chairs, put plastic sheeting on the floor under the wall which was to be knocked through, move Reggie's perch to behind the counter, and take down the little curtains and lamps so that they didn't get all dusty. Flora decided to pop the curtains through the wash at home, to make use of the time when the tearoom was closed to do a bit of a spring – or autumn as it was – clean.

"Perfect," Flora said, as they surveyed the now-empty space, just as Adam's phone rang in his pocket.

Flora tried hard not to overhear Adam's side of the conversation, but it was difficult when he was standing right next to her. She busied herself making sure all of the plastic sheets were weighted down, but all of Flora's senses were on alert when she heard Adam mention her name.

"And what does this mean for Flora? Surely you don't mean to bring her in again today, it's pitch black outside," Adam said, his tone angry. He listened for a response from the other end and then said, "Very well, tomorrow at ten, yes I understand, thanks McArthur." Adam ended the call, his eyebrows drawn together and the wrinkles marked on his forehead.

"Let's go back to the coach house, love," he said, trying to guide Flora to their coats gently.

"No, wait, I want to know what that call was about," Flora stood her ground, wanting to put her hands on her hips but stopping herself at the last moment, "I gather it was McArthur giving you some inside info?"

"I think it'll be best if we talk when you're sitting down at home…really, trust me," he added, rather worryingly Flora thought.

"Very well," she gave in reluctantly, and they wrapped up to head out into the dark night. Supper time had been and gone, but they were both evidently still full from Betty's cake as neither even mentioned food. They left the car at the tearoom and hurried along the footpath that cut across to the coach house. Adam had tried to hold Flora's hand, but she pretended not to notice, and instead rushed ahead of him. It was churlish, she knew, and she certainly didn't want to be taking anything out on the man, when he had been nothing but supportive, but Flora couldn't help herself. She was down to her last nerve and wasn't sure she could take any more this day.

"She's a corker! My Flora!" Reggie squawked happily as they entered, spraying a load of seeds onto Flora's head as he flew onto her – evidently they had caught him snacking from the bowl on his perch!

"Good bird," she said, absentmindedly, as she and Adam shed their coats and went straight into the sitting room. Thankfully, the log burner was still giving off some warmth, and Flora was glad of it. She felt chilled to the bone.

"So, spill," Flora said, when they were both sat down. Adam looked uncomfortable perched on the edge of the sofa, as if he had the weight of the world on his shoulders.

"Well, love, I don't want you to get upset... or angry, but McArthur said they've been in contact with Gregory's girlfriend – a Ginny Pendlebury-Muse."

"Ex-girlfriend, according to him," Flora cut in, though she wasn't sure why.

"Ah, well, she seems to still be sharing the same address as Mr. Temple. Anyway, she is flying up to Newcastle, will be here very shortly apparently, and is going straight to the police station in Morpeth."

"And why would that make me angry or upset?" Flora asked, confused.

"Ah, well, that would be because Blackett spoke to her briefly on the phone and she told him that the last time she spoke to your ex was when he was on his way out of the village in his car – with you!" Adam's raised eyebrows, which asked the unspoken question for him, were his only comment on that.

"With me? But I was never in his car! Why would she

say such a thing?" Flora felt a ball of panic and anger lodge in her chest, and rubbed the spot ineffectually through her jumper to try to get rid of it. Her voice had risen about an octave and she realised she was sounding shrieky.

"That's the million dollar question, isn't it, love," Adam said, pausing as if giving Flora a chance to admit to anything.

"You do believe me, don't you?" Flora could feel the tears building in her eyes once more, and tried desperately to control them.

"I do, yes," Adam sighed, "but why would she say that? It doesn't make sense. Anyway, McArthur says they want to interview you again, as soon as they've taken a written statement from Miss Pendlebury-Muse, so you're to be at the station in Morpeth by ten tomorrow. They'll phone you directly to confirm this, though. I'm not officially allowed to be a go-between."

"That's fine then," Flora bit out, "I'll drive straight there after I've spoken to the builders about the next stage of the conversion works on the stables."

"I'm really sorry I can't drive you, but we shouldn't be seen together by my colle..."

"I understand. Really." As much as she loved his company and valued his support, Flora simply wanted to be left alone now with Reggie to collect her thoughts, for what she imagined would be a gruelling day ahead. Even if he had been allowed, Adam could not help her with that, so after a few uncomfortable minutes she asked him to leave.

"Are you sure? I can stay a while longer," he seemed wary of leaving her alone.

"No, I'll be perfectly fine. A bubble bath and bed for me, I think," Flora said resolutely, though she felt anything but.

"Okay, well I'll call you first thing and meet you at the tearoom whenever you get back, so that we can get started on the decorating," Adam said, reaching across to cup Flora's cheek with his hand.

Flora pulled away and stood up abruptly. She was well aware that she was pushing away the only one who could really help her, but nevertheless she stuck to her guns. Forcing back the tears, she said a stilted goodbye to Adam, though the cottage seemed empty and her heart even more so when Bramble reluctantly took his leave and walked back down the path in the rain to collect his car from the tearoom.

ELEVEN

The next day dawned cold and damp, but thankfully without the downpour that the villagers had come to expect from this November. Flora had to force herself out of bed, her eyes stinging from lack of sleep and her head pounding from the same. She took some painkillers and tried to avoid looking at her reflection in the mirror as she got ready for the day. Choosing a sombre trouser suit in charcoal tweed and a grey matching blouse, Flora rushed to grab her phone from the bedside table when she heard the ping of an incoming message. Hoping it would be from Adam, she was almost disappointed to see that it was instead from Harry – an email containing pictures of he and Betty at the airport, huge smiles on their faces.

Normally, the sight would have brought a mirroring smile to Flora's expression, but not this day. Today, she simply sent back a smiley emoji and then swiped the message away.

She had spoken to Ted Charlton about the building works scheduled for the week, and was just setting off on her way to Morpeth when Adam eventually called through the Bluetooth device linked to her car.

"I'm sorry it's so late, love, I just wanted to wait for any updates before I phoned you," he said, the apology clear in his voice.

"No worry, I'm on my way to the station now. Did you... did you hear anything?" Flora didn't want to ask, but couldn't help herself.

"Only that they've got the statement from the girlfriend, and have also interviewed that school teacher who saw you with your ex."

"Phil? Oh. Okay. Well, I guess I'll just see what they say when I get there."

"Keep your chin up love, you've done nothing wrong. Don't act guilty."

Flora wasn't sure exactly what that meant, but she ended the call as politely as possible and tried to focus on her driving. As she passed the scene of Gregory's crash, and saw that the car had been towed away but that the police tape remained, Flora was thankful that she had chosen to skip breakfast, as it would surely have made a reappearance about now. She ploughed on, worried what the morning would reveal.

As she pushed open the door to the police building, Flora was faced with Phil Drayford, leaving. Their eyes met and both registered shock, with Phil muttering, "I'm sorry, Flora," as he rushed past her. Obviously, this did little to fill Flora with any confidence, so she announced her name at the desk with a certain amount of trepidation in her voice.

It was forty-five minutes later, when Flora had sat alone in the interview room, staring at the same peeling walls, that Blackett and McArthur deigned to join her.

"Mrs. Miller, thank you for agreeing to attend once again," Blackett began formally, reeling off the same list of warnings and information about recordings and evidence as he had the previous day. Flora listened, her face impassive, until Blackett finally sat back, laced his fingers together on top of the table, and stared straight at her with his cold, calculating eyes.

"So, Mrs. Miller," it was McArthur who began the

Absence Makes the Heart Grow Fondant

questions this time, "some further evidence has come to light since we last spoke and we now have reason to believe that you were in the car with the missing man, Mr. Temple, just before the crash. Indeed, you may well have been with him during the RTA. The blood on the passenger seat is being tested to see if it matches Mr. Temple's, which we believe to be a rare type, and if not, then we will see if it matches your own. Can you explain what happened in the vehicle?"

"No," Flora said flatly.

"No?"

"No, because I was not in the car with Mr. Temple, at that time or any other since our divorce."

"That is strange. Especially as we have a witness who says they spoke to Mr. Temple and is adamant that he said you were with him. That being quite apart from the fact we found your necklace in the footwell of the passenger side – a necklace you have already confirmed as belonging to you."

"Did this witness see me? Hear me?" Flora was trying to hold her nerve as best she could, though she could feel her hands shaking on her lap, "I have already explained how the necklace could have fallen off when I first searched the vehicle. My wool coat was not fastened at the front you see, it just had a belt and ..."

"Please answer the questions, Mrs. Miller," Blackett interrupted, "Why were you in the car, and at what point did you get out?"

"I was not and therefore I did not," Flora said, keeping her tone even, "I only looked in the car when I found it abandoned."

"Very well, we will return to that later," McArthur continued, "now, we have a reliable witness who says they saw you arguing with your ex-husband the day before his disappearance, is that correct?"

"Yes."

"Pardon, please speak up for the tape."

"Yes, Gregory, ah Mr. Temple, came to my door and we had words about his reason for visiting me. He left and that was the last I saw of him."

"Oh come on, Mrs. Miller, it was more than just 'words' was it not?" Blackett asked, leaning forwards in his chair opposite Flora.

"It was a disagreement, unfortunately witnessed by Mr. Drayford," Flora said, before clamping her lips together so that she said nothing more that might incriminate herself. She worried that they would twist her words and use them against her.

"So, you have 'words' and then you end up in your ex-husband's car either that evening or the next day, a car which crashes off the road and into a wooded area from a cause unknown, and the driver of said car is not here to tell us what happened. All very convenient, do you not think, Mrs. Miller?" Blackett said, his voice almost a sneer.

"Nothing about this situation is convenient," Flora felt her temper rising and tried to keep her voice sounding normal, "and again, I was not in the car when it crashed."

"But just before?" Blackett ploughed on, like a dog with a bone.

"No, not at all, not at any point," Flora clarified once again.

They went on like this, around and around in circles for the next hour or so, until Flora felt tired and confused with it all. She explained all three of her conversations with Gregory once again, and then how she had found his car, but nothing she said seemed to convince the two detectives, who simply looked at her with blank expressions the whole time. Eventually, in the early afternoon, Flora was allowed to leave, and hurried to her own car on legs that felt like jelly. She had not been charged or cautioned, but neither did Flora feel that she had been believed. She was definitely still under suspicion, and had been told in no uncertain terms that she was expected to be available at all times to help with further enquiries.

The only development in the case which would possibly help her, it seemed, would be the re-appearance of Gregory himself, and Flora was determined to do what she could to find the man, regardless of Adam's warnings to not get any further involved than she already was. Heading back to Baker's Rise, Flora decided that she would look through her old contacts in her phone that evening and see if she couldn't do some digging of her own.

TWELVE

After a quick cheese toastie with Reggie at the coach house, and a change of clothes to some old leggings and a faded sweater suitable for decorating, Flora set out to meet Adam at the tearoom. The bird unfortunately had to be left at home, as the dust and rubble from the knocked-down wall would be too much for him, a fact which Reggie lamented the whole time while Flora was putting on her boots and coat.

"Welcome to the tearoom," he squawked on repeat, as if showing Flora just how good he could be!

"I know, you're a great help, but it's not safe in there for you this week, while the tearoom's closed," Flora replied, ruffling his head feathers and feeling slightly silly that she was explaining herself to a bird.

The wind was getting up again, and a mixture of fallen, brown leaves and twigs dislodged during the storm whipped up around Flora's ankles as she rushed along the little path, trying to avoid the puddles. Adam's car was already outside the tearoom when she arrived, and she found him inside the new conversion talking to Ted Charlton. The team had already brought down the connecting wall and were making good the opening between the two areas. Flora's happiness at seeing her ideas come to fruition was hampered by the thick cloud of suspicion and worry which hung over her, so she simply thanked Ted and moved to the far end of the room to begin preparing the area for painting.

"Flora, love, how are you doing?" Adam asked quietly, following her.

"As well as can be expected. Have you heard anything else?"

"No, nothing."

"Well, can we just not mention it then? And just get on with the jobs?"

"Okay, but Flo…"

"Please Adam, just leave it!" Flora was already on the verge of tears, and moved away to give herself some space to get them under control. The last thing she wanted was for the builders to see her in a state.

"Okay, well, why don't you pop through and make us all a cuppa, and I'll start getting everything ready," Adam said gently, respecting Flora's need to focus on the task at hand, "Ted says they'll be done in here by tomorrow afternoon, then they can move back up to the big house and get on there, plastering the walls that have been messed up by the new installations. That's great news, isn't it!"

"Yes, I suppose so," Flora couldn't muster up the necessary enthusiasm, though she knew it meant the bookshop could be opened at the start of the new year if she hurried. She left Adam without further comment and went through to the tearoom end, picking her way through the builders who were working on the new opening. Sometimes it felt like all she did was make hot drinks for people, but Flora knew she shouldn't complain. It was light years away from her old job in the City – so much less stress and fewer hours, no commute, no patronising businessmen to deal with… The thought gave Flora an idea, and she resolved to phone Gregory's closest business partner in the investment firm the pair directed as soon as she got a chance.

The builders had finished up for the day and Flora was just tidying the paints to put away until tomorrow, when she heard a car pulling up outside. Flora stretched her back, which was protesting at the sudden and unusual exercise, and peeked out of the window hole which the builders had made and covered with a transparent plastic sheet, ready to be filled with new double glazing later in the week. Flora didn't recognise the car, but she did recall the woman who was now getting out of it. The leggy, twenty-something blond was no other than Gregory's former PA and most recent girlfriend, Ginny Pendlebury-Muse.

"What on earth can she want?" Flora asked no-one in particular, "And after lying to the police as well! I'm going to have it out with her!"

"Flora?" Adam came over from washing the paintbrushes in the tearoom sink just as Flora was disappearing out of the door.

"Ginny, isn't it?" Flora asked before the woman had reached her, trying to take charge of the situation, even if neither her body nor her mind felt up to the confrontation.

Absence Makes the Heart Grow Fondant

"Yes, Ginny Pendlebury-Muse," if she was taken aback by Flora's forthright approach, the younger woman didn't show it, perching precariously in her three-inch heels on the gravel, "And you are Flora Temple."

"Miller now, actually," neither of the women reached out a hand to shake. In fact, they stood about two feet apart, eying each other warily, "and you are Gregory's ex-girlfriend?"

The emphasis was on the 'ex' and Flora caught the hint of red which blossomed over Ginny's cheeks as she answered, "Yes, yes, of course, ex-girlfriend," stumbling over the words.

"This is my friend Detective Adam Bramble," Flora volunteered, indicating Adam who had come to stand just behind her, and again emphasising the Detective in his title.

Ginny's face blanched now and she looked as if she really wished she hadn't come, wringing her hands and looking from Flora to Adam and back again.

"You arrived very quickly from London, Ms. Pendlebury-Muse," Adam phrased it as a statement rather than a question, in his best professional tone, fixing her with his stare.

"I, ah, I, well I flew up, yes."

"Very lucky to get a seat, what with all of those who couldn't fly North during the storm being moved onto later flights," again, Adam spoke as if it were purely a comment, but they all knew there was a serious undertone, "and then to hire a car and find Morpeth and this little village. You must be an experienced traveller."

"Well, I used to go to the Med with Mummy and Daddy in school holidays, and then Gregory and I went to the Amalfi Coast last year," Ginny stopped speaking when she realised what she had said – she had travelled abroad with Gregory when he was still with Flora.

Flora wasn't shocked, it merely confirmed her suspicions that not all of her ex-husband's 'golf trips' had been just that. She really couldn't have cared less at this point, but was enjoying making the younger woman squirm, "I imagine you have shared many lovely things with him, I'm quite surprised you are no longer together, in fact, especially since you are still ensconced in the Kensington house," Flora said pointedly, before they descended into an uncomfortable silence again.

"So, what can we do for you," Adam asked, "You must

have sought Ms. Miller out for a reason?"

Ginny swallowed three times in quick succession, as if summoning up the few tears which filled her eyes, making them round and luminous, "I'm looking for Gregory, I've been distraught since the police called me yesterday, where can he be?" she wailed the last part, an effect which Flora thought could earn her a job on the stage, "He told me you were in the car with him, Mrs. Miller, then the call went silent."

"We both know that is not true," Flora said harshly. If the younger woman was expecting her to play along, in any way, shape or form, then she'd had a wasted journey, "if you have come to spread your lies, then you might as well leave."

Ginny blinked away the tears quickly, and her expression took on a harder edge, "The man could be dead!" she said, holding the back of her hand to her forehead in dramatic fashion.

"You should not jump to conclusions, Ms. Pendlebury-Muse," Adam said, in a tone harsher than any Flora had heard him use previously, "there is more at stake here than your expensive holidays and designer clothes, much more, and false accusations serve no-one."

Ginny took a couple of steps back, nearer her car door which was still open, "I shouldn't have come," she said petulantly, clearly annoyed that Adam had implied she might be shallow!

"Quite right, you should not. On that, we can agree," Flora said, turning away and disappearing back into the tearoom.

Adam stood and watched as Ginny got into her hire car and drove off, her face a picture of anger at having been so summarily dismissed. He was proud of Flora for her steadfast refusal to acknowledge the younger woman's pleas – her acting skills were certainly worthy of an Oscar – but he wondered if sending her off with her tail between her legs wouldn't perhaps lead her to act out even more. He could only hope that Blackett would see through her lies. His colleague was clever and astute, but had been known to be swayed by a pretty face and a comely body in the past, despite his dour outward appearance. Adam sighed and turned back to the tearoom, feeling that his hands were tied and wishing there was more that he could do.

THIRTEEN

Adam found Flora on her phone, leaning on the counter in the tearoom. She had a look of displeasure on her face, and he could hear the ring tone on the other end.

"Hello?" A gruff voice answered.

"Jeremy Hampton?" Flora asked.

"Yes, who is this?"

"Jeremy, it's Flora, Flora Mi... Flora Temple as was. How are you?"

"Flora? Well, long time no speak. What can I do for you? You haven't seen Greg have you?" the man sounded hopeful, rushing to his last question.

Flora was surprised that he would mention Gregory so soon in the conversation, as politeness dictated they make odious small talk first. Flora wasn't disappointed – she wanted to get this call over as quickly as possible – but it did strike her as unusual.

"That's why I was calling actually, to see if you had heard from him?"

"No, I have been trying to get hold of the man, myself, he has been avoi… missing my calls for a week now!" Jeremy sounded frustrated and, to be honest, rather angry, leading Flora to wonder what had happened between the two men who were usually such buddies. Not only partners in their investment firm, Gregory and Jeremy were like two peas in a pod, competing with each other to chase deals and women, always interspersed with a few rounds on the golf course and some drinks at the nineteenth hole.

"Oh, I see, well, sorry to have bothered you," Flora was keen to end the awkward phone call.

"Wait! Flora, I haven't seen you around since the divorce. Around London, I mean."

"What? Oh well, it is a rather big place! But that would

actually be because I've moved up north."

"Up north eh? Is it as grim as they say?" Jeremy phrased it as a joke, but Flora wondered what he was fishing for.

"No, actually, it's lovely."

"And what part of 'up North' would that be exactly? Does Greg know where you are?"

Flora felt uncomfortable and her instinct told her not to give the man too much information, "Ah, north of Newcastle-upon-Tyne," she answered vaguely.

"Well, that's almost in Scotland!" Jeremy's false joviality was really starting to grate now.

"Anyway, good to talk to you, bye Jeremy."

"Sorry I couldn't be of help..." his voice trailed off as Flora hung up. A shudder ran through her, and she turned to Adam who was standing just behind her.

"Need a hug, love?" Adam opened his arms and Flora walked into them. It felt good to snuggle up to him.

"I'm sorry I was so... so snippy earlier," she whispered.

"Don't be silly, I understand," Adam spoke into her

hair as he kissed her head lightly.

"Thank you. I thought I could track down a lead, a clue, anything, by phoning Gregory's business partner and best friend, but if anything it's just made me feel even more unsettled."

"Maybe leave it to the professionals, hey?" Adam said it gently, without any hint of reprimand, and Flora was grateful for the sweet man that he was.

"We should clean up and get these clothes in the wash before the paint dries on them," Flora changed the subject, "Do you want to come back to the coach house?"

"No love, if you don't mind I'll head home and get myself sorted. I'll be back first thing tomorrow to report for painting duty, though!" He tipped Flora's chin gently so that he could angle in for a kiss.

A sigh escaped Flora's mouth as his lips touched hers, and she wished that they could forget about all of the nonsense and just be together for a while. It was too difficult while there was this cloud hanging over them, though, and she knew Adam was right to give her some space to process things in her head. Wasn't that just what she'd wished for the previous evening?

"Bye, love," Flora pulled away and used Adam's regular term of endearment for her. *Did she love him?* she wondered suddenly. She had a sneaking suspicion she might.

Flora waved Adam off and hurried along the path to the coach house, hearing her phone beep in her handbag. She pulled it out, before her keys, when she reached the front door, to see another email with more pictures from Harry and Betty – plane food, view from plane window, several similar shots – as they were flying to Florida, where their cruise was to depart from Fort Lauderdale. Flora sent a quick note back, wishing them a safe journey, before letting herself into her little home. Part of her wished she was off on holiday right now, anywhere away from this place, then she chided herself for being so ungrateful. A flash of green heralded Reggie's arrival on her shoulder as Flora deposited her handbag and headed straight for the shower. She had much to be thankful for, she knew, but everything felt like such an effort at the moment. Not least because she was a suspect in a potential death investigation.

Freshly showered and changed into some thick, lined trousers and a pretty blue sweater, Flora's stomach grumbled loudly. She was dismayed to see that there was little in either her fridge or cupboards that would constitute a meal – Adam had used the last of the pasta and sauce yesterday, as well as the few mushrooms, onions and small block of cheese that Flora had. She didn't keep her kitchen very well stocked, there being just herself to think about normally and it being such an inconvenience to drive to a big supermarket, but Flora had to admit that she needed something to eat this evening, especially after the energy she had expended at the tearoom. It was already dark outside – the sun was fully set by five o'clock in mid-November here – so Flora had no choice but to rush down to the village and grab something from Baker's Rise Essential Supplies before Jean closed for the evening.

"I'm sorry, I have to go out again. I won't be long though," Flora apologised to Reggie, something which came naturally to her now – she spoke to him as if he were her housemate!

Reggie cocked his head to one side and waddled to and fro along the back of the kitchen chair. Flora looked lovingly at her typewriter and her neatly typed sheets of children's stories which were stacked in a clear wallet next to it. She knew that she needed to be in the right headspace to create another epic tale of Reggie's adventures, and that time probably wasn't now, not today anyway. Flora hoped, however, that when the bookshop was open and the police had located Gregory, with his disappearance being long forgotten, then she would be able to do some readings of her stories, maybe from professionally printed books. The thought gave Flora a warm feeling – not quite happiness, there were too many unresolved things going on for that – and she took a moment to enjoy the thought before reluctantly pulling her coat and boots back on and heading out into the dark.

FOURTEEN

Thankfully, the light in the local grocery shop was still on, and Flora hurried inside out of the cold.

"Flora, you look frozen through!" Flora had to do a double take when it was not Jean, whom she'd expected to see behind the shop counter, but rather Tanya who greeted her. She was wearing a lime green knitted dress, which Flora saw came down to her ankles when her friend came around to hug her. She had on house shoes, had her red hair tied up in a multicoloured scarf and wore her signature red lipstick. A typical 'Tanya look' Flora thought, slightly envious of her friend's confidence and ability to pull off every outfit!

"Tanya! How are you? Is Jean okay?" Flora looked around the tiny shop but saw no sign of the other woman.

"Yes, she needed to pop upstairs to take a pie out of the oven, so I said I'd step in for a moment. I only came to buy some milk!" Tanya laughed, and Flora realised how good it felt to speak to her friend, "You look pale, Flora, I hope that ex-husband is not still bothering you?"

"Well, there's a story there, but it'll take a while to explain. Do you want to come up to the tearoom tomorrow morning? It's closed and Adam and I are decorating the bookshop, but I could do with a chat."

"Of course," Tanya smiled as Jean joined them.

"Thank you Tanya, oh hello Flora! You're just in time, I was about to close up for the evening. Would you two ladies like to join me upstairs for a cuppa? These winter nights can get lonely when you're old like me!" Jean winked and Flora laughed.

"That would be lovely," both Tanya and Flora said in unison, as Flora grabbed a few groceries. Once these were rung through the till, Jean changed the small sign on the door to 'closed', locking them in, and they went up the back stairs to her apartment above. As Flora could have predicted, the place was cosy and beautifully decorated, with little china ornaments, and cushion covers which Jean had obviously knitted herself. A large, black cat with a white patch of fur around one eye snoozed on an armchair. Other than opening one eye when they entered the room, he didn't move a muscle to welcome the visitors.

"That's Smudge, he tolerates me living with him," Jean said, once they were sat at her small table with cups of tea and slices of hot apple pie with Cornish clotted cream, "have you heard from Betty and Harry?"

"Yes, they've been keeping me updated on their journey with lots of photos," Flora said, bringing her phone out to show the two women, "I imagine there'll be many more where these came from when they actually get aboard the cruise ship!"

"I'm so happy for them," Jean said wistfully, "since my Thomas died I've missed having someone to share things with."

Tanya reached out her hand and put it over Jean's, "Well, we are always here if you want a natter."

"Thank you, I have my customers to keep me busy during the day, of course – that's mostly the reason why I haven't retired yet. At seventy-four, I should probably let someone younger take over!"

"You don't look a day over sixty!" Tanya exclaimed and Jean blushed at the compliment, "Of course, if you're looking for something to keep you busy in the evenings for the next few weeks, you could always put your name up for the village talent show," Tanya suggested, a cheeky gleam in her eye.

"Well, I don't know how to do much other than knit, crochet and bake," Jean said thoughtfully.

"Ah, but can you speed knit?" Tanya asked.

"Speed knit?"

"Yes, you could show everyone that you're starting at the beginning of the show, then sit at the front and knit a hat in the shape of a Christmas pudding or something," Tanya giggled, "then you could produce the finished item at the end of the show!"

"Well, I am a dab hand at hats," Jean said, laughing with her, "leave it with me and I'll think about it!"

"How is the list looking for auditions?" Flora asked, "I'm sorry I haven't been much help yet, Tanya."

"No need to worry, I have it all in the hand. Will is going to do some animal jokes, Shona and Aaron are doing a superhero mime act at the beginning of the show, before Shona rushes back to tend the pub for opening night, Lily and Stan are bringing some real animals, my Pat will be playing his classical guitar and I think Edwina Edwards fancies herself as an opera singer or some such… anyway, we will have enough people, I think. Oh, and Billy Northcote mentioned he had written a poem about roses, dedicated to his late wife, so that should be lovely. To be honest, the auditions are really just a formality, I'm going to include everyone and then we can get started on rehearsals. Are you free on Friday nights?"

"Well, I hope so, if they don't lock me up in the meantime," it had come out before Flora realised what she had said, and she saw the shocked faces of the two women opposite her.

"Is everything okay?" Jean asked softly, "or was it just a figure of speech because you have a lot on your plate at the moment?"

Jean had given her a get-out clause, but Flora saw no point in not sharing with her friends. She had done nothing wrong, after all, and knew they wouldn't gossip around the village, "Well, it started with the unexpected appearance of my ex-husband, Gregory…" Flora began slowly and soon she was spilling all of the recent days' events. It felt good to get it all out, cathartic even, and afterwards Flora was glad she had confided in them.

"That's ridiculous!" Tanya said, in her usual blunt way, "They can't think you had anything to do with it! Maybe he banged his head in the accident and has amnesia, and the fool wandered off, or maybe he just went for a piddle in the woods and got lost!"

The women laughed, and Flora admired Tanya's ability to break the tension.

"Yes," Jean added, "he may have been kidnapped by faeries or have decided to join a travelling circus troupe who saw him on the road!" They all shared their most absurd possibilities then, and it cheered Flora's heart. Although they were being silly, it did bring home the point that there were many other options as to what had happened to her ex-husband, which did not involve anything sinister. Flora just hoped that something could be established and proved soon, so that she wouldn't have it hanging over her.

More tea and pie followed, meaning that Flora had no need to cook when she got home. Instead, she had a long soak in the bath, followed by some time teaching Reggie new phrases.

"I'm a star!" Flora said slowly, "I'm a star!"

"She's a star!" Reggie said, happy to have Flora home and to himself.

"In a book," Flora said, "in a book!"

"Look! Look!" Reggie squawked.

"No, book, book" Flora repeated. It was nightly routines like this that kept her anxiety at bay and helped Flora to try to think positively. She didn't always succeed, but between time spent with Reggie, her friends and Adam, she felt better this evening than she had for days. Adam had promised her that without a body, the police would have trouble building any kind of case against her, and Flora hoped that this would be true. Even more, she hoped that Gregory would re-appear, as if by magic, and put an end to the whole stupid charade. Anyway, it was a much more relaxed Flora who went to bed that night, planning to get up early the next day and visit the manor house before meeting Adam and Ted Charlton at the tearoom. Life must go on, and Flora knew she would just have to deal with whatever it threw at her.

FIFTEEN

It was freezing in the big house on top of the hill the next morning, and Flora was thankful that the new heating system was installed so she could finally heat the old place up. The heating engineer was now doing his final checks, the rest of his team having finished up and moved onto a job in another property. The plumber and electrician's teams had also just completed the rewiring and piping, and Flora was expecting a couple of hefty invoices in the next day or so. With Reggie on her shoulder, Flora took a slow tour of the downstairs rooms. Her heart sank a little when she saw the holes in the walls which had been made in order to fit the new wires. There was so much for the building team to make good in these rooms before they could be decorated. Free of all of Harold's papers, at least Flora could see the full size of the spaces now, and the thought of how they could look did still fill her with excitement. She trailed her hands along the wooden dado rails and over the china cabinets, knowing she would need to decide soon which furniture to keep and which to send to charity or auction. Certainly, before the rooms could be painted and have new flooring laid, they would need to be cleared. Sometimes the list of jobs felt overwhelming, though Flora knew there was no real rush to complete them. It was her own impatience that made the project feel stressful. Well, that and the fact that every small job seemed to cost a fortune.

Returning to the kitchen, where no renovations had yet taken place other than Flora adding a new perch she'd had delivered the previous week for Reggie, she took a moment to enjoy the view from the large windows. Bleak and wet, it was still a calming scene, and one which Flora drank in. A flash of a dark green cap caught Flora's eye, and she was surprised to find Billy Northcote already up there, sitting on his bench in the rose garden. Rushing out to greet her friend, Flora brought him inside with her for a hot drink. Poor man looked frozen. At least Flora had a kettle and some teabags up here now.

"Billy, you'll catch your death of cold if you sit out there."

"Aye lass, but I'm getting on a bit you know, it might be my last year to sit and see the seasons change. This time of year was my Mabel's favourite, when she could sit inside with the fire on, doing her knitting and listening to the radio. A real homebody she was. But she loved coming up here and watching me work in the spring and summer months. She would sit on that bench there, her knitting needles clicking away, and we'd share a flask of tea and a scone during my break."

"Oh Billy, to love and be loved like that is a very special thing," Flora felt suddenly very emotional and busied herself making the drinks.

Reggie sat on his perch, chirping away and bobbing up and down happily, and Flora joined Billy on the other rickety old stool at the breakfast bar, reminding herself that she really did need to get a proper table and chairs for this room. The old gentleman looked uncomfortable perched on the wobbling seat.

"Mrs. Miller, would this be a good time to show you how to work the boiler, thermostat and the like?" The heating engineer, Chris Bewick, poked his head in from the narrow corridor which led to the laundry room.

"Oh, yes, excuse me, Billy," Flora followed the man out of the room, down the few wooden steps and into the large space which would hopefully soon be filled with a washing machine and dryer as well as new counter tops and cupboards. When Flora finally got around to choosing a style for the kitchen, she would have it matched down here. She was certainly planning to keep the traditional wooden pulley drying rack which hung over their heads, a Sheila maid it used to be called, Flora remembered reading. As well as being practical since it was very much still usable, the piece brought a hint of the house's history to the room, which Flora loved. She was keen to keep as many of the traditional features as possible.

As Chris pointed to buttons and dials, and then suggested they go to see the water tanks housed in the attic, Flora was distracted by the sound of Reggie screeching and Billy shouting. Surely the pair would not be arguing? It was completely out of character for Billy, and Reggie had been so happy and calm when she left the room. For her to hear it from down here, Flora knew the kerfuffle must be pretty loud.

"Excuse me Chris," Flora was already on her way out of the laundry area, "I must just see what…" Her heart was beating erratically as Flora ran up the tiny staircase, even more worried when she realised that everything had suddenly gone silent. Pushing open the heavy wood door to the kitchen, Flora let out a shout of dismay when she saw Billy lying on the floor of the kitchen, his hand over his chest.

"Billy, my goodness, Billy," Flora flung herself down onto the floor next to the old man, laying her hand over his, "Chris, Chris can you help me?" she shouted over her shoulder.

Billy's eyes were wide open, unseeing, but when Flora leaned close to his mouth she could feel a very slight breath coming from him, "Billy, what happened? Chris call an ambulance!"

Billy blinked once and returned Flora's squeeze of his hand with a tiny movement of his own. Then he looked directly into Flora's eyes and his mouth turned into a whisper of a smile, "Mabel..," he whispered, on a long exhalation, and then he was gone.

"No! No, no, no," the tears were streaming down Flora's face and she squeezed Billy's hand again. No response came, and she hadn't really expected it to. Flora moved her hand up to the man's wrinkled face and cupped his cheek. Leaning over him, she placed a soft kiss on his forehead. In the background, Flora could hear Chris speaking to the emergency services operator, but Flora couldn't move. Frozen to the spot, she rested her forehead against Billy's, praying that he was with his Mabel, together for eternity now.

The village was quite a way from the nearest hospital or ambulance depot, and the ambulance seemed to take an age to reach them. Flora sat on the floor with Billy, refusing to leave him. Chris had said they probably shouldn't move him and Flora agreed. Instead she simply closed the man's eyes and sat with her hand on his arm, as if he could still feel her close to him and providing a sense of comfort. Flora knew that she was really only trying to comfort herself. She knew that it didn't matter how long the paramedics took, they wouldn't be able to save him. As her eyes drifted from Billy to the window and then the door, Flora noticed a trail of muddy footprints leading into the room. She was sure they hadn't been there before, as Billy had taken his dirty boots off before coming into the house, leaving him in his stockinged feet. The sight of his big toe sticking through a hole in the wool now brought a fresh bout of sobbing, and Flora brushed her hair back from her wet face.

Chris hovered nearby, intermittently going to the front of the house to look out of the window and check for the ambulance. Flora heard her phone ringing, and forced herself to stand to grab her handbag. Her legs, long-since numb, protested at the movement and pain shot up into her back.

"Flora? I'm at the tearoom, love, ready for the decorating. Did you sleep in?"

Flora's crying ramped up at the sound of Adam's reassuring voice, "No, no, I'm up at the big house. Can you come up here? Quickly? There's been an..," Flora couldn't speak.

"Yes, love, I'll see you in two minutes," he rang off without further question.

Flora sank back down, only then realising that something was wrong. Other than her friend being dead. Other than her heart breaking in her chest. The room was too still, too quiet. Looking up to Reggie's perch, Flora realised for the first time since coming back into the room that the bird wasn't there. Reggie was gone.

SIXTEEN

From being so still and quiet, there was a sudden flurry of activity in the room as first Adam arrived and then the ambulance crew. Adam didn't ask any questions at first, simply took in the sight of Flora, and the body on the floor, and immediately knelt down beside Billy, feeling for a pulse and then laying his coat over the old man's top half. As he did so, Flora garbled out the shouting she had heard, and pointed to the footprints in mud on the kitchen floor. Without speaking, Adam whipped out a tape measure that he must have had hidden about his person and measured the size of an individual footprint, before taking photos of the muddy imprints on his phone. He then looked at Billy's feet in only his socks, to Flora, in her leather boots, and then over to Chris Bewick who stood in one corner, looking pale.

"What size shoes are you?" Adam asked, looking at the man's work boots.

"Ten."

"Would you mind if I take a closer look and quickly measure the sole?" Adam walked towards the other man, who complied without quibbling, "The prints over there have a distinctive circular mark at the heel."

Flora was relieved to see Adam in full police mode, taking charge of the situation. She certainly couldn't think straight, her hands shaking and the tears still rolling down her face, silently now. It was a good job he acted as quickly as he did, for when Chris led the paramedics in a few minutes later, the footprints were covered with fresh mud tracks. By this time, Flora was in Adam's arms, having a brief hug before she pulled away to answer their questions. Adam phoned in the incident, given that Flora had heard shouting before Billy collapsed, and they were soon joined by Pat Hughes and his trusty German Shepherd Dog, Frank. A beast of an animal that was all muscle, and had officially retired from the Police Canine unit in Newcastle with an array of medals, before being gifted to Pat to spend his retirement patrolling the small village. Although his air was menacing, Tanya had told Flora that he was a softie at heart. Flora watched as the dog began sniffing around the room, his ears alert and all of his senses working. Flora wrung her hands in worry, as she wondered if the dog could detect more than drugs and contraband. *Did he have any experience with searching out parrots?* she wondered, before realising that was a ridiculous notion.

"Why don't you go and search for Reggie, love," Adam suggested, and Flora knew he was trying to encourage her to leave the room, "he probably just flew into another room in fright. He always loved the front sitting room when he lived here before, didn't he?"

Flora nodded silently in response, leaving quietly and walking down the wide hallway. She went into the study first, having a good look around and finding nothing amiss. Her heavy feet then led her to the main front room, which looked exactly as it had earlier. No sign of a little green parrot anywhere.

"Reggie, Reggie good boy," Flora called, clicking her tongue against her mouth in an impression of the bird's own clucks.

The only sound was the muffled voices coming from the kitchen. A ball of ice lodged beside the grief which had already settled over Flora's chest, and she began to panic in earnest.

"Reggie, Reggie!" Flora looked behind the curtains, under the tables and in the cupboards, anywhere a little bird could hide. Nothing. Moving to the dark dining room, Flora pulled open the old velvet curtains at a side window, getting a face full of dust for her trouble. This room had not been too badly affected by the rewiring, with just a few holes in the wall, which did not detract from the hideous animal heads which Harold had festooned around the room. Flora shuddered at the sight of them, and recalled why she could count on one hand the number of times she'd been in this dingy area of the house. There was no sign of Reggie, and Flora made a quick exit, pulling open the door under the stairs, where she had found her typewriter, as she hurried back to the kitchen. It was still squeezed shut, so there was no way Reggie could have become trapped in there, but Flora opened it anyway. It showed nothing different, other than the two new electrical control boxes that had been installed.

Feeling defeated, she returned to the kitchen, where Doctor Edwards was kneeling over Billy's lifeless form, and Adam stood deep in conversation with Pat.

"Aye, I'll take a look at the security footage with Flora

now," Adam was saying quietly as Flora came to join them, "there's no cameras in the house, but it'll show anyone approaching outside."

"What's your verdict, Doc?" Pat asked, as the physician straightened up.

"I can't be sure, it could just be old age of course, but I'm thinking heart attack. Could he have had a shock or something?" the doctor directed his question to Flora, and all eyes were suddenly on her.

"Well, I heard shouting, could that have caused it?" Flora asked, trying to stop her lip and chin from quivering.

"Well, yes, it's possible, or a struggle of some kind," Doctor Edwards ventured.

Flora put her head in her hands, and felt Adam's arm come around her shoulder, "Come on love, let's leave them to it. Where do you keep the CCTV monitor?"

"In the study," Flora said quietly. It was actually in the secret room, where she had found Harold's hideous files, but she didn't want that to be public knowledge, so she simply led Adam through. Behind them, she heard Pat Hughes begin questioning Chris Bewick. The poor man had only come to finish the heating job and now he was caught up in all this. Flora herself had had enough of police questions to last a lifetime.

"So, let's have a look then," Adam said once he and Flora were ensconced in the small space, with the door propped open slightly as Flora still hadn't worked out how to open it from the inside. Adam expertly rewound the footage from the morning and they both watched, eyes transfixed on the screen. Flora sat on the large office chair, with Adam leaning over her shoulder as the images from the morning came up. Adam had his finger on the fast forward button and they scrolled through slowly, until they saw Flora walking up the driveway with Reggie in his little case, and around the side of the house. A few moments after she had entered, a hooded figure approached from the same direction, crouching down behind the bushes on the other side of the path, observing the side door.

"Oh my goodness!" Flora whispered, "there was someone following me!"

Adam rewound the tape to see if they could get a better look, but the tall, slim figure was dressed all in black, with their hood pulled low over their face, so there was nothing to give away their identity. They were holding something under their arm – a box maybe? Adam scrolled through quickly again, until they saw Flora coming to the door and calling for Billy to join her, then the pair made their way back into the house. The figure did not move for a few minutes, but then ran across to the side of the house, hugging close to the shadows on the side of the building, then creeping down to peer in the side window to the hallway. They stayed, waiting there, until several minutes farther on in the tape, where they could be seen entering the house itself. Flora felt the tears fill her eyes as she realised that's when she must have gone from the kitchen with Chris, leaving Billy and Reggie alone. A minute or so later, the intruder left, carrying the box, and ran off the way they had come.

"Well, that's our culprit, I'd bet my life on it," Adam said gravely, "and if I'm not mistaken, I'd say that box has Reggie in it!"

"Oh no," Flora couldn't hold back the tears any longer, and rested her head on Adam's chest as he crouched beside her, "what should we do?"

"I'll pass all of this information to Pat, see if he can review it and let us know if he recognises the individual on the tape. He has a much better local knowledge than me. In the meantime, we can ask around the village, in case anyone's seen anything, or heard an angry bird!"

"My poor Reggie!" Flora wailed, feeling pathetic and helpless.

"Come on love, let's get you back down to the tearoom. I can finish up with Pat here and make sure it's all locked up. I let Ted Charlton and his crew in this morning with the key you gave me the other week, in case of emergencies. So, why don't you see how they're doing – they should be almost finished by now – and you can get yourself a hot drink and a sit down."

"I don't want to lea…"

"Flora, love, they will have taken Billy now. His soul is hopefully at peace, and I promise we'll find out what happened here, and get Reggie back. I give you my word."

"Thank you," Flora kissed him quickly on the cheek, before standing and making sure the secret room was closed behind them. With a strength she didn't feel, Flora walked purposefully back to the kitchen, gathered her coat and bag, and left without saying a word to the local policeman. Her composure was held in place by a fragile thread, and she knew that even one kind word would break the tenuous control she was fighting for.

SEVENTEEN

Flora ran down the hill to the tearoom on shaky legs, and arrived there breathless and panicked. On entering the small building she could hear the familiar voice of Ted Charlton, talking to another she recognised – Tanya. It had completely slipped Flora's mind that she had invited her friend round to the tearoom for a cuppa and a chat, but she had to admit to being very happy to see her.

"Flora!" Tanya exclaimed when she saw her, "I came up as you suggested yesterday, but if you're busy we can rearrange," she looked closely at Flora's face then and took her by the elbow, gently leading Flora through from the converted bookshop area and into the main body of the coffee shop itself.

"I'm okay," Flora whispered, though they both knew that was a lie.

"You don't look okay, Flora, please sit down," Tanya pulled the plastic sheeting back from a stack of chairs and lifted one down for Flora to use, "there, now catch your breath while I put the kettle on."

Flora sat still on the edge of the seat, not even removing her coat or the bag from her shoulder. She heard the builders whistling as they did the finishing bits and pieces behind her, smelt the fresh paint, heard the kettle coming to life, and felt Tanya lifting another chair from the pile. Flora herself, however, felt disconnected from the whole scene, her eyes unseeing and her senses muted, so transfixed was she by the images of the morning which flitted through her head.

"Flora, Flora," Tanya was rubbing her arm now. Flora looked up to see the other woman holding out a cup of tea. On autopilot, she accepted the proffered drink and took a tiny sip. It was very hot, and sweet – too sweet, really, but Flora knew that Tanya was trying to help calm her nerves.

"So, where is our little feathered friend?" Tanya asked, obviously hoping to distract Flora and lighten the mood. Unfortunately, it had the opposite effect, and Flora began weeping anew. It wasn't Tanya's fault, of course, she wasn't to know the effect the reference to Reggie would have, but she looked immediately regretful.

"Oh, Flora, I'm sorry, has something happened? Is he with Will at the vet surgery?"

"No, no, I ah..," Flora took a deep breath and put her cup down on the floor, there being no table that wasn't stacked and covered.

"Take your time," Tanya said gently, her eyes kind and her tone patient.

"Thank you. Well, there has been a tragedy..," Flora told Tanya about Billy, and how her husband Pat was up at the house investigating. Tanya couldn't hide her shock, and her own sadness, and both women ended up crying together. Billy had been a much-loved member of the village, and everyone had a soft spot for the man.

"Oh Flora, that is awful. I have no words," Tanya snuffled, when they had both run out of tears.

"And that's not all," Flora continued, when she felt she could form a sentence again, having taken a big gulp of

Absence Makes the Heart Grow Fondant

her tea which had now cooled considerably, "I think Reggie has been birdnapped!"

"Birdnapped? No! By the guy who you saw on the camera?"

"I think so. I wonder if he thought he could just sneak in and grab the bird, but then saw Billy and they had words. Or worse, maybe he hurt Billy? Pushed him or something?" Flora's voice rose in desperation, "I imagine the old man would have stepped in if he saw someone trying to grab Reggie. It's my fault, I shouldn't have left the room."

"Don't be silly, Flora, you couldn't have known! We will have to speak to my Pat and your Adam," Tanya said decisively, "the bloke couldn't have gotten far with Reggie, if they were in public someone would have noticed. We need to start looking for him right away. Besides, it will do you good to be busy and pro-active," Tanya added, sagely.

"It will," Flora agreed.

The two women were just leaving the tearoom, to walk back up to the manor house, when a large black car skidded to a halt beside them, sending gravel flying.

"What on earth?" Flora exclaimed, she really wasn't in the mood for any more unexpected occurrences today. Her stomach fell even further, when she recognised the short, thick-set man who levered himself out of the vehicle.

"Jeremy, I did not expect to see you here," Flora said curtly, eying Gregory's business partner suspiciously. For him to drive all the way up from London, and so quickly, must mean he had an urgent need to find Gregory, or to at least find out more about his disappearance. He was looking rather unkempt, in sharp contrast to his usual pristine appearance.

"Well, we can't have our Greg missing, can we?" Jeremy said, his voice rough and hoarse, which Flora knew to be a side-effect of his thirty-a-day cigarette habit, "How are you bearing up, Flora?" He eyed her swollen eyes and red face distastefully.

She wasn't bearing up well at all, but it had nothing to do with the disappearance of her ex-husband and everything to do with the death of a friend. Flora had no intention of explaining that to this particular man, however. Indeed, her instinct was to send him on his way as quickly as possible.

"I haven't seen Gregory, and I've told the police all I know," Flora said tersely, "perhaps you should go and speak to them in Morpeth. You've had a wasted journey here. How did you even find me?"

"Quick search on the internet and I found press coverage of your summer fete. I'm sure we could have a drink and a proper catch-up," Jeremy said, his eyes flitting to admire Tanya in her leopard print mini skirt and high pink heels, as he licked his lips in a decidedly off-putting manner, "I'm sure if we go over it all something will spring to mind!" He acted as if he thought Flora knew more than she was saying about Gregory's disappearance, which only served to irritate her further.

"I'm busy, Jeremy, as I'm sure you are too," Flora's tone left no option for debate. For the second time in a week she wished to goodness that she had never given that interview for the local media.

"Right you are. Oh, you haven't seen Ginny, have you?" Jeremy added the question nonchalantly, but Flora noticed his expression harden for a moment. She recalled that he and Ginny had had a fling before she had moved onto Gregory.

"I have, but only briefly. Whether she's still in the area I don't know," Flora said, turning her back on the man and walking away, her arm linked with Tanya's.

"Who was he?" Tanya asked when they were far enough away to not be overheard.

"Best friend and business partner of my ex-husband. There's something odd going on with them," Flora answered, thoughtful, "I'm sure he didn't know this part of the country even existed until now. The Jeremy I know would certainly never make a trip up here voluntarily. Not if it wasn't serious!"

"Well, he seems like a snake in the grass," Tanya said, eying Jeremy's car over her shoulder as it made a hasty exit.

"I think you could be right there," Flora agreed, as the two women hurried back up to the main house.

"Alright love," they met Pat on his way back down. He put his arm around Tanya's shoulder and pecked her on the temple. She smiled back up at him. Frank pulled on his leash, eager to get back to some action.

"Have you any more information?" Flora asked, hopefully.

"No lass, nothing that you didn't already hear. You'll need to avoid going in the big house for the moment, until I get word from above whether they want to do a full sweep of the room for evidence, or whether it's to be put down as natural causes."

"Oh. Okay then," Flora swallowed heavily, "I'll just look around the grounds for Reggie then."

"Aye, that's what Bramble is up to now, having a good look around. The land around the estate is so extensive though, it'll take a team to search in every nook and cranny. I'm heading back to the village to phone everything in and write up my notes."

"Did Adam show you the CCTV footage?"

"Yes, and it doesn't give us much to go on, I'm afraid – some bloke of medium build, with his face covered. Could be any one of a number of people," Pat was rather too vague for Flora's liking.

"But what about Joe Stanton? There was all that suspicion around him before, when I got the threatening note through the door."

"Have you had any more of those since?"

"No, but I…"

"Well, just leave it to the professionals, eh lass? I did speak to Joe at the time, and of course he denied all knowledge, but he didn't hide his animosity towards you, so there may be something in it. I'll seek him out again today."

"Thank you, Pat," Flora felt dissatisfied, but she couldn't push any further.

"Chin up, Flora," Tanya gave Flora's arm a reassuring squeeze as she waved her husband goodbye, "let's go and find your birdie."

"Okay then," Flora replied, rather desolately. The block of ice in her chest was even bigger now, threatening to engulf her, and Flora felt permanently on the verge of tears. Her worry for Reggie, mixed with her grief for Billy, was a weight almost too heavy to bear.

EIGHTEEN

They found Adam in the rose garden, sitting on Billy's bench, and fingering the man's thermos flask which had been left on the ground there. His expression was grim, and Flora wanted nothing more than to snuggle into him, to try to ease her aching heart. With Tanya alongside her, though, she held back and instead simply greeted him from a foot away.

"Flora, love, are you okay? Any sight of Reggie at the tearoom? Maybe he flew somewhere he recognised?"

"No, nothing, just another unwelcome visitor," Flora quickly explained the bare bones of Jeremy's visit, and Adam noted the name and a few details in his notebook, to pass on to McArthur.

"Have you been back to the coach house to search?"

Adam asked.

"Oh no! I didn't think of that!" Flora's eyes filled with tears when she realised she'd overlooked the most obvious place for Reggie to retreat to.

"Don't worry, we can go there now," Tanya said hastily.

"Yes, yes, let's," Flora replied, "then we can search the village."

"I'll stay and look around up here, in the trees and bushes lining the lawns and gardens," Adam said, cupping Flora's cheek briefly, his eyes meeting hers and conveying a promise of hope.

"Thank you," Flora fought to speak past the lump in her throat, "let's text each other when we're finished and meet back at the tearoom. Or let me know straight away if you find anything."

"Aye, that I will," Adam gave her one last reassuring smile, before turning and heading round the back of the manor house.

"Come, let us hurry down the hill and find that cheeky chappy," Tanya said, trying to sound more enthusiastic than she felt. Flora was glad of her friend's company as they rushed back the way they had come.

The coach house was exactly as Flora had left it – *was that only this morning?* It wasn't even lunchtime yet, and she felt she had lived through several days' worth of emotions. She had secretly hoped to find the sweet parrot waiting for her on the doorstop, but sadly that was not the case, and Flora's heart fell. Unlocking the wooden front door to let them both in, Flora was met with silence. She knew that Reggie couldn't have got back inside of course, but when she wasn't met with the usual flapping of wings and arrival of her little feathered friend, his absence really hit home and Flora had no option but to let the tears fall again. Sometimes it felt like all she had done recently was cry.

"Oh Flora," Tanya gave her a hug, and Flora dried her eyes quickly, not wanting to succumb to a full-blown weep.

"Let's leave our bags and look around the outside of the cottage," Flora said, "then we'll have a quick cuppa and a toilet break and head into the village."

"Sounds like a plan!" Tanya agreed.

The search of their surroundings brought no clues and the two women were preparing to head into the village after a quick refreshment break, when the doorbell rang.

"Oh!" Flora said hopefully, "Maybe that's Adam, or someone else with Reggie!" Her heart racing in her chest, and hope bubbling up, Flora threw open the front door. To her dismay, it revealed the dour faces of Blackett and McArthur.

"Mrs. Miller," Blackett said gravely, "May we have a word?" It was phrased as a request, though they all knew that in reality Flora had little choice but to comply.

"Well, I was just looking for Reg…"

"It will only take a minute, there has been a development," McArthur added ominously.

"Very well," Flora sighed heavily, as they followed her into the small kitchen where Tanya was waiting.

"Ah, alone would be preferable, Mrs. Miller," Blackett said, rather rudely.

"I will go and look around the tearoom once more," Tanya said, ignoring the officers and looking directly at Flora, "then you can meet me there."

"Thank you Tanya, yes I won't be more than a few minutes," at least Flora hoped that would be the case.

"Bramble tells me you have suffered an additional loss this morning," McArthur began when they were all ensconced in the small sitting room, "my condolences."

"Thank you," Flora whispered, not trusting her voice not to crack. She held her head high and looked at Blackett directly.

"Well, Mrs. Miller, the lab analysis has come back confirming the blood on the passenger seat was indeed that of your ex-husband. This puts a slant on the case that is rather more serious, as you can imagine," Blackett's beady eyes bored into her, but Flora did not flinch under his scrutiny.

"That is worrying, from the point of view of your case, I can understand that," Flora began, "and of course I would not want anything bad to have happened to him, but other than a general care that any normal person would have, I retain no personal feelings for my ex-husband." Flora chose her words carefully, not wanting anything she said to be latched onto and twisted.

"But you admit you were the last to see him," McArthur interrupted.

"I don't know that, and neither can you," Flora said, mentally praising herself for her ability to stay clear-headed under current circumstances, "I know nothing about his actions or his whereabouts after he left my home on Saturday evening."

"Yet his former girlfriend, who felt so worried that she herself made the journey up here at an instant's notice," Blackett's voice had an ominous quality, "has said in a formal, signed statement that you were in the car with the man just before the crash."

"Well, we only have her word for that, don't we?" Flora said, looking Blackett directly in the eye in a silent challenge.

"We do," McArthur cut in, "which is why we are grateful to you for helping us with our enquiries."

"Very well, but I have nothing further to add. The blood is a worrying development, from an investigative point of view, I can see that," Flora said decisively, "but I have no further information to add, that I have not already told you both several times. Now, I must be getting on. I believe my parrot has been birdnapped."

"Birdnapped?" Blackett parroted back to her, his tone scoffing.

"Indeed," Flora stood and made to direct them to the

door.

"We will be in touch, Mrs. Miller, please keep yourself available," McArthur added as the pair left. Closing the door behind them, Flora finally let out the breath that she felt had been suffocating her throughout their whole visit. If things could get any more complicated then she wasn't sure how! *But then,* Flora noted regretfully, *I've thought that in the past and sadly been proved very wrong!*

NINETEEN

Speaking into her mobile phone as she rushed down the path to the tearoom to find Tanya, Flora quickly told Shona and then Lily Houghton about poor Billy. Both were equally shocked and Flora invited them to the coach house for afternoon tea. She felt that having her friends around her, where they could all share their grief, would not be a bad thing. Flora was learning that there were distinct benefits to living in a small community, which far outweighed the negative feeling of living in a goldfish bowl where everyone knew each other's business. She planned to also invite Amy and Jean, and the vicar's wife, Sally. Having forgotten to cancel her bakery deliveries for the week of the tearoom's closure, in true Flora style, she had plenty of cakes to serve to her friends!

Flora was proud of how she had dealt with the visit from the two detectives, and intended to try to tap into this confidence in her search for Reggie. Tears would serve no purpose other than giving her another headache. Tanya had found nothing new, not that Flora had really thought she would. The realisation was slowly sinking in, as it became more apparent, that Reggie had been deliberately taken. If he were free, he would have been either in the big house or at the coach house or tearoom. Flora knew he would never disappear completely of his own free will. They would search the village, calling into all the shops on Front Street to ask if anyone had spotted the bird or, indeed, anything unusual, but Flora did not have high hopes for making any progress as to Reggie's whereabouts. She hoped that Pat, and his trusty sidekick, Frank, would have more luck. She had given Reggie's carry case to the policeman so that his dog could have a good sniff and get the bird's scent.

Flora's phone pinged as she and Tanya were coming out of the hairdressers, having invited Amy to the afternoon tea in memory of Billy, and she grabbed it from her bag quickly hoping it was Adam. Instead, it was another email from Harry and Betty, containing a file attachment which held a couple of dozen pictures of the cruise ship, their berth and balcony, the formal restaurant… and so it went on. Flora didn't even bother to flick through them all, swiping the message away to reply to later. She certainly didn't plan to tell the couple that Billy had passed away, not until they returned to the village. They deserved to have a proper honeymoon, and Flora was determined not to put a damper on that.

"Is there news?" Tanya asked, her tone hopeful.

"No, nothing about Reggie or Billy," Flora replied, wishing fervently that she could say otherwise.

"Shall we pop in to ask my Pat what headquarters have said about Billy's death? I'd like to know if they're going to investigate it," Tanya said.

"Yes, that's a good idea, then we can drop into the vicarage and let the vicar know, assuming of course that he hasn't already heard," Flora added, "and invite Sally for afternoon tea. I could do with my friends around me."

"And we're all here for you, and for each other," Tanya squeezed Flora's elbow where their arms were linked.

As Flora had predicted, their search proved fruitless.

Pat told them that Billy's death was being treated as suspicious, so Adam was going to let the forensics team into The Rise, and a copy of the security footage was also being passed over for analysis. Flora felt comforted that this was being taken seriously. She owed it to Billy to make sure that his passing was investigated, to ascertain once and for all whether it had been anything other than natural. He may have been well into his nineties, but he had seemed fit and well when Flora had spoken to him, if not just a little melancholy.

"Tis a sad day, indeed," Jean said when the women were all gathered in Flora's sitting room, tea and scones served all round, "I have known Billy since I came to the village, and that was almost fifty years ago now. A good friend he has been to me, and to many, especially when we lost loved ones. Betty will be heartbroken when she hears, though I understand why you don't want her to find out while they're away, Flora."

Flora nodded sadly, "it will be strange not to see him up in the rose garden. I'll have a plaque put on his bench in his memory. A tribute to him and Mabel."

"Aye," Lily agreed, "he wasn't a stranger up at the farm either, often popping in to have a good old natter with my Stan." She wiped her eyes surreptitiously.

"He was like a grandad to me," Shona tried to hold back the tears, "and to Aaron."

"He will be missed, that's for sure," Tanya added.

"I didn't really know him, having just come to the village recently," Sally said, "but my James will give him a good service to send him off. I'm sure he's already up there with his Mabel, watching us all fretting and shaking his head. He's in a happier place, I'm sure."

The women all agreed, and Amy stood up to pass the carrot cake around. Flora noticed that she was quite a shy young woman when she wasn't talking to you one-to-one in the hairdressers, but she always had a smile, and a gentle presence.

The talk moved to the funeral, to Billy's sons – who must be in their late sixties or seventies by now – and then Flora heard the sound of something coming through the letterbox.

"Excuse me a moment, that'll be the post. I'm expecting some book catalogues for the new bookshop," she added, leaving the room and walking down her tiny hallway.

Panic and dread filled Flora simultaneously as she spotted the envelope on the doormat. She recognised the blank white rectangle, with only her name on the front, immediately. Ignoring it, she stepped over the offensive missive and pulled the door open quickly, eager to catch sight of whoever had shoved it through her letterbox. No such luck, the perpetrator had disappeared again.

"All okay?" Sally asked, as she came halfway down the hallway to the kitchen door, the large teapot in her hands for refilling.

"No, ah, actually it wasn't the postman," Flora said quietly, the envelope in her shaking hands. She realised then that she should have picked it up with a sandwich bag the way Adam had with the original threatening note, received over a month ago. She was annoyed with herself for forgetting, and rushed to the cupboard to get a bag, even though she doubted the police would find any fingerprints on the letter – they certainly hadn't last time.

Flora had an idea what the message would say even before she opened it. Sally stood beside her, a worried expression on her normally cheerful face.

"Flora? What is it? This looks a bit ominous!"

"It is, I've had one before," Flora whispered, though there was no hope of keeping the delivery secret. All of the women had squashed into the tiny kitchen now, come to see what was keeping the two so long.

Flora pulled the letter out of the envelope carefully with her 'gloved' hand. Just like last time, it was a message of only a few lines, made up of magazine cuttings.

"I have your bird. Pay up and leave the village or he's a feather duster!" Tanya read loudly over Flora's shoulder. The sum of £10,000 was added underneath.

"Oh my goodness!" Amy and Jean said simultaneously.

Flora felt her knees go weak and clutched the counter for support.

"Let's get you sat down," Sally said kindly, as the paper fell to the floor, "and we can contact Detective Bramble. He'll know what to do."

"Aye," Lily said, "someone's playing silly beggars and we'll all help to find out who!"

Adam arrived ten minutes later, a sheen of sweat on

Absence Makes the Heart Grow Fondant

his brow from rushing down as soon as Tanya had called him. Flora was back in the sitting room, in her favourite armchair, being fussed over by the other women.

"What's all this love?" he asked gently, coming to kneel beside Flora's chair.

Flora simply handed him the letter, her hand still encased in the sandwich bag, "here, see for yourself," she said bluntly, not trusting herself to speak more.

Adam took the threatening missive in his own winter-gloved hand and studied it for a few seconds, a frown deeply ingrained on his forehead.

"Flora says it is not the first," Tanya spoke up.

"Aye, I was here when she received the other note. There were no more to follow, so I hoped your husband's warning had been enough to scare the man off." Adam's voice was almost a growl and his hand shook like Flora's – though from anger in his case.

"Do you mean Joe?" Jean asked.

"Aye, I can't think of anyone else, and Pat said he acted all shifty like when he questioned him about the last letter. He must've been biding his time. No it's him all right, but Pat phoned to say there's no sign of him at his cottage or anywhere else around the village. He's gone to ground, to be sure."

Flora rubbed her hands over her tired face, feeling drained and washed out. She needed time to grieve for Billy, she needed to get back to the decorating in the bookshop, but above all she needed her little bird back. Thoughts of his cheeky, feathered face brought to mind the pet portrait that Flora had commissioned back in September. She had the idea to contact the artist, Lizzie, to ask her to email the photographs she had taken of Reggie on their first visit so that Flora could quickly mock up a poster to put up around the village, asking everyone to look for Reggie. This, in turn, reminded her of Harry's many photos from the cruise ship, and that she must reply to his email.

"Flora love, you're in your own little world there," Adam rubbed her shoulder gently.

"Sorry, just… so much to think about."

"Aye, I know, and I imagine you're in a bit of shock too. I'll get off and speak to McArthur and then Pat Hughes again. You let me know if you hear anything, and I'll meet you at the tearoom again later."

The women also gathered their coats and bags, and headed out to look for Reggie, with Flora moving as if on autopilot. Her legs felt heavy, her head as if it were filled with cotton wool, and she felt not even a spark of hope in her chest.

TWENTY

The following days passed slowly, the dank, miserable weather reflecting Flora's mood. Everyone in the village was looking for Joe Stanton, and for Reggie too, thanks to the posters which Flora had put up all over the place. Adam had been loathed to let her out of his sight, and Flora had caught him looking at her worriedly on more than one occasion as they painted the new bookshop. Not least, Flora surmised, because her appearance had become a rather startling outward expression of her inner turmoil. Not just because she was wearing old clothes for decorating, but also because her unwashed hair was perpetually scraped up in a messy bun and her eyes more often than not showed signs of recent crying. Flora had asked the building crew to leave the big house until the New Year, as she couldn't face making decisions up there right now. Whenever she thought of the place, her mind automatically drifted back to Billy and she felt the grief of his loss all over again. Arrangements were being made for his funeral, to be held the following week, and Flora expected the village church to be packed with all the locals who were lucky enough to have called him friend.

All thoughts of Christmas and the village talent show had been pushed to one side, as Flora simply did not have the head space to deal with anything extra at the moment. Between her worry for Reggie, her grief for Billy, and the manual labour she was doing in the bookshop, Flora had enough on her plate. At least, by evening time she was too exhausted to dwell too much on anything. Thankfully, Tanya had stepped up to the plate and taken over the organisation of Baker's Rise Stars in their Eyes, seemingly happy to have the role, which was certainly a weight off Flora's shoulders.

It was on one of her lunchtime trips into the village – ostensibly to buy more sugar, as Adam took three spoonfuls in each hot drink – but in reality, to look for signs of Reggie, that Flora stopped short when she rounded the corner onto Front Street. There, leaning up against the front façade of the still-closed pub, was Jeremy. What on earth he would still be doing hanging around the area, let alone the village itself, Flora had no idea. She herself was thankful not to have had any more visits from the dour detectives concerning Gregory's disappearance.

With his back to her, and unaware of her presence, Jeremy spoke with some agitation into his mobile phone, "Yes, I told you, there's no sign of him! Him and the money, both vamoosed!... The police? These local grunts are useless, hardly the Met I can tell you! What?... No! I can't go back to the wife, they're divorced and she'll get suspicious – always was a quiet one, that one, judging you with her eyes! I reckon she knows a lot more than she's saying... did the police suspect? I doubt it, as I say they couldn't organise a party in a brewery. I told them I was there out of friendly concern... what was I meant to say? That Gregory did a load of dodgy dealings behind my back, secretly bankrupted the company, and took what was left from the business account before running into the back of beyond?" Jeremy raked his spare hand through his greasy hair before shoving it into the pocket of his winter coat and pulling out a half empty packet of cigarettes, "Anyway, gotta go Mike," Jeremy hastily ended his call when Shona emerged from the Bun in the Oven, little Tina on the lead behind her.

Jeremy turned to move away, and in doing so caught sight of Flora who was hurrying across the road behind him.

"Flora! I didn't see you there!" he rushed to catch up, and had his hand on Flora's elbow before she could get far enough ahead of the man. As Flora turned, she caught Jeremy looking her up and down with evident distaste, clearly thinking that her appearance had gone downhill considerably since leaving London.

"Jeremy, what a surprise! I was just hurrying to the corner shop, actually. Sugar," Flora added unnecessarily, "I have to dash!"

"Actually, Flora, I'm glad I've met you, any sign of the chap himself?" they were on the opposite side of Front Street now, the little row of shops all lit up against the gloom of the day. Some had even started decorating their windows with festive lights and trees. Flora wondered if she'd ever feel festive again.

"Gregory? No," Flora didn't feel like elaborating.

"Nothing from the police?" Jeremy squinted his piggy eyes together and studied Flora's expression closely. His jowls jiggled from the movement, his skin sagging and mottled from many years drinking and living the high life.

"I really must dash, Jeremy. I'm surprised to see you

still here, surely you should be in the office?" Flora caught the red flush which spread up the man's neck, and knew her comment had hit home. From what she'd just heard during his phone call, he didn't have much of a business to go back to. When she'd been with Gregory, the investment firm had been thriving and extremely profitable, so it had taken a nosedive indeed. Thoughts of nosedives reminded her of her little bird, and Flora had to swallow back a lump in her throat as she left the man standing where he was, his mouth round like a fish swallowing water.

She hurried to catch up with Shona who was a few feet ahead, and waiting for Flora on the pavement.

"Shona! How are the preparations going for the pub's grand re-opening in December?"

"Very well, thanks, Will has been helping me redecorate the place while Aaron is in school during the day, bring it a bit more up to date, you know. I was hoping to speak to you, Flora, actually, I keep meaning to pop up to see you."

"Oh?" They paused outside the shop that had been in the making to be Baker's Rise Candy Surprise, until the owner's real identity had been exposed.

"Yes, I ah, well, I know that Emma Blenkinsopp kitted

out some of this little shop before she was arrested for my dad's death, and I was wondering if I could buy some of the shelving off you? I want to add more storage to the basement, make it lighter and... well, as I know you'll understand, I find it difficult to go down there after what happened, so Will suggested a bit of a facelift in there too might help?"

"Great idea, and you can have whatever you want from in here for free," Flora said, rummaging in her handbag for the set of master keys which Harry had given her before going on holiday, "Emma didn't pay any deposits, so the place was never officially hers. No time like the present, let's take a quick look now, shall we?"

Shona put little Tina back on the ground, as she had scooped her up into her arms whilst the two women were talking. The little dog was barking excitedly, and Flora wondered if she thought they were going to take her home to Betty's. Flora unlocked the door and flicked on the lights. The place still smelled of fresh paint and the pink colour which covered half the walls seemed garish against the glare of the bare lightbulbs.

"Here we are," Flora said, gesturing to the small space with a sweep of her arm. Tina tugged and tugged on her leash, until Shona gave up and simply let go of it.

The little dog shot off into the back room, where Betty had lain injured during the awful showdown with Emma, and Flora suddenly thought she understood the dog's haste – perhaps she was checking that her owner wasn't still in there, given that she didn't understand that Betty and Harry had gone on holiday. As the two women tried to discuss which of the shelving units Shona could use at the pub, they were interrupted by an incessant yapping. Constant and high pitched, it become impossible to talk over.

"Tina, what is it?" Shona asked, raising apologetic eyebrows at Flora and following the little dog into the back area, which housed the stairs to the upper flat. Tina stood at the bottom of the staircase, something distinctly green in her little mouth.

"What is that you've got, Tina?" Flora asked, bending down to have a closer look, "My goodness! It's a feather! A green parrot feather!" Tina continued her yapping, with the small feather stuck in the corner of her mouth. Shona gasped and brought her hand up to cover her mouth, stopping any further sound from escaping.

"Quick, text Pat!" Flora whispered, as she herself brought out her phone and typed a swift message to Adam. Shona picked up the tiny dog, who was reluctant to leave, and the two women backed out onto the street again, Flora quickly locking the door behind them.

TWENTY-ONE

"Did you not want to go upstairs and see if Reggie is there?" Shona asked, her eyes wide.

"Not yet, not if who I think may be hiding with him is also there, it's best to wait for either Pat or Adam. There's no other way out but through this door. I can only think that he was given a copy of the door key from Emma, without either me or Harry knowing," Flora was mostly muttering to herself now, hopping from one foot to the other impatiently, "I hope he didn't hear us and is hurting my Reggie!"

Thankfully, they didn't have long to wait, as both Pat and Tanya arrived from the direction of their house, Frank pulling on his lead as if he could smell the excitement. Flora, who was holding the feather now, let the big dog have a good sniff of it.

Absence Makes the Heart Grow Fondant

"That was a cryptic message, Shona," Pat said, out of breath from the effort of reaching them so quickly, his large midriff jiggling under his police tunic, "something about an emergency at the sweet shop here?"

"Yes," Flora answered him, "Tina found a green feather inside, and since Joe Stanton was close to Emma Blenkinsopp I wonder if he's hiding out upstairs?"

"Right!" Pat's eyes gleamed at the opportunity of an actual arrest – a rare occurrence in this village before Flora showed up!

"Let my Pat check it for us," Tanya said, rubbing Flora's arm through her winter coat.

Flora unlocked the door and Pat let Frank take the lead. The burly canine rushed through the front part of the shop without pausing and straight into the back. Flora desperately wanted to follow, but knew better than to get involved in another tricky situation. Instead, she was relieved to see Adam running around the corner by the pub.

"Sorry, love, I didn't hear the message come through, had the radio on too loud. I only checked my phone when I realised you'd been gone far too long. What's happening?"

"Reggie and Joe are maybe upstairs in the flat. Pat's gone to see," Flora said quickly, her stomach churning and the bile rising into her throat to make speaking uncomfortable.

"Right you are," Adam said, and darted inside without another word.

The three women and little Tina waited impatiently on the street for what seemed like twenty minutes, but which was probably only actually four or five. A light drizzle had started, which blanketed them all now in its heavy dampness. Eventually, the men emerged. Pat and Frank first with Joe, who had his hands handcuffed behind his back, and a rather ragged, bite-shaped hole in the bottom of his trousers. Frank held the piece of torn material in his doggy mouth like a badge of honour. Joe's head was adorned with what could only be described as livid, red peck-marks, and Flora was glad her little guy had stood up for himself. Behind them, Adam followed with a shoebox, from which much angry chirping could be heard.

"Reggie!" Flora exclaimed, wishing she could push past Joe and Pat to get to him.

"I should've wrung his scrawny, green neck when I

had the chance!" Joe snarled at her, "Here's me thinking you'd pay up, you stingy cow! You ruined my life, you bitc…"

"That's enough of that, you're in quite enough trouble as it is!" Pat said, taking Joe to where a squad car had just pulled up on the opposite side of the road, its blue lights flashing.

Back at the coach house, the fire on, and Reggie where he belonged nuzzled into the crook of her neck, Flora let out a huge sigh of relief. He was home, and relatively unscathed from his ordeal, though decidedly angry and looking thinner. Flora had fussed around her little feathered friend, preparing him a fruit salad of gargantuan proportions, which Adam said he himself would have no hope of finishing, let alone a small bird!

"So, what was up there, in the apartment?" Flora asked, when they were both sitting with a well-earned cup of coffee.

"Stupid fool was hiding in a wardrobe, as if we wouldn't check! That big dog – Frankie is it? – Well, he sniffed him out straight away. Joe had Reggie here in there with him, and the bird was going bananas pecking at him," Adam smiled at the memory, "In his holdall we found the magazine clippings for more messages, so that's the evidence we needed that he was the one threatening you. Nothing to prove whether he hurt Billy though, but I told Pat to tell the station that they should check the soles of Joe's boots to see if they match the prints I measured and photographed up at the big house. If they have the distinctive circle pattern on the heel, that would also indicate a match."

"Take that, you old codger!"

"Pardon me?" Flora looked at Reggie in startled amazement, moving him to her hand to look into his little face, "say that again, Reggie."

"Take that, you old codger!" It was the first sentence the little bird had spoken since his return, as he had restricted himself to angry screeching and then contented chirping since his release from Joe's hands.

"Do you think he could have heard Joe say that to Billy? I've never heard him use those words before," Flora wondered.

Adam already had his trusty notebook out – always in his trouser pocket, even when he was off duty. He was due to go back on duty the next day, though not to work on the investigation into Gregory's disappearance, and Tanya would help Flora with the last day of finishing touches and clearing up in the bookshop ready to open the tearoom again on Monday.

Adam noted down the phrase, with a look that was part amazement, and part excitement, "I'm not sure that it'll hold up as evidence, but if we tell Joe we've got a witness – without letting on who it is – it may be enough to get him to talk!"

"Good bird!" Flora snuggled in closer to her little buddy and felt some of the strain of the week drain from her. Now all she needed was Gregory to turn up alive and well, and everything could go back to normal before Christmas.

Apart from Billy, of course, he wouldn't be there to read his poem for Mabel in the talent show as planned. Flora felt guilty for having, for a brief moment, not felt her usual pain about his passing and his coming funeral, so happy was she to be reunited with Reggie. Tears filled her eyes as the grief hit her again, mixed this time with guilt.

"If I hadn't invited him in, if I hadn't left the room," she began, as Adam came to put his arms around her. Flora snuggled her head into his broad chest and let the tears fall, "I'm sorry, you'd think I'd be all cried out by now!"

"Don't be silly, it's going to take a while for you to get over this, it's been quite an ordeal. But as for thinking silly things like those 'what-ifs', believe me, I've had a lot of those in my life and in the end they're a pointless waste of your energy. We can all ask, 'what if?' but it doesn't change anything," Adam's words were harsh but true, and Flora tried to stop the whirring in her head of all the things she could have done differently. She knew that she needed to move on, to focus on making the tearoom festive for its reopening on Monday, to try to find a normal routine again, it just seemed like it was all shrouded in sadness right now.

Flora's phone pinged and she wondered if it would be Pat with an update from the station. Instead, it was another email from Betty and Harry, this time detailing a day trip to St. Thomas in the Caribbean with another attachment of photos. Flora felt awful that she had forgotten to reply to their previous three messages, which had been coming in every day without fail. Showing Adam the beautiful pictures, Flora felt a moment of jealousy – *some sea, sand and sun would go down a treat right now*, she thought, as the rain hammered against the windows of her little cottage, and the draft wafted the flames in the fireplace.

"Aye, looks lovely," Adam said wistfully, and Flora imagined he was thinking much the same thing as her.

"Maybe we could have a break in the spring time?" Flora asked, wishing as soon as the words were out of her mouth that she hadn't been so presumptuous as to assume they'd still be together then.

"I would love that, Flora," Adam said, cupping her chin and kissing Flora gently.

"My Flora! She's a corker! You sexy beast!" Reggie screeched in quick succession, flying up to his perch and eying their closeness with a look that, if he were human, would have been one of mild disgust.

The shock was enough to have Flora and Adam jumping apart like teenage sweethearts who had just been caught kissing by their parents, and the two laughed as Flora tried to hide her blushing cheeks.

TWENTY-TWO

Flora surveyed the little tearoom, set back to rights with all the tables arranged in their usual positions again. She had put a small curtain up between the bookshop and the tearoom for now, as the new area wouldn't be open until the new year. Tanya had helped her at the end of the week to get the tearoom scrubbed down of all the dust, and then to decorate it for the upcoming festive season. With fairy lights around the door and windows, bows made from red velvet (an old curtain from the manor house which Flora had dry cleaned in the summer for this very purpose) which were pinned to the wall and a small artificial Christmas tree, adorned with lights and baubles, it looked pretty as a festive picture. The normal white tablecloths and doilies had been exchanged for red and green, and the usual crockery changed to a Christmas set which Flora had found in the china cabinets up at The Rise. All in all, it looked like a miniature version of Santa's grotto, though perhaps rather more tasteful, and Flora couldn't have been happier with the final result.

Tanya had flatly refused any payment for her work, so Flora offered her first choice of any vintage women's clothes found up at the big house when the bedrooms were cleared in January. Flora herself had wondered if there might be some old Christmas ornaments and the like up in the huge attic, but she hadn't been able to face going up to explore yet. Everything up at the manor house had been put on the back-burner until the new year, when Flora hoped she would have the head space for it all once again. Right now, it felt as if she were simply juggling too much. Reggie sat on his perch in the corner, where he had been throughout the whole of the cleaning and decorating process, as Flora couldn't bear to have him out of her sight at the moment. She knew he wasn't at risk, as Joe was in custody now, but her anxiety still needed to keep her feathered friend close.

Adam had called to say that Joe would be charged for the theft of Reggie and for the threats against Flora, but he hoped they would also have enough evidence to prosecute for at least manslaughter, if not a lower degree murder for Billy's death. As soon as he was told about the 'witness,' Joe had apparently pleaded for a deal if he spilled the truth about what had happened with Billy. Adam had not gone into details, and Flora knew he was trying to spare her further upset. She wasn't sure if she was grateful or not – perhaps knowing the facts would make it easier? In any case, the man would be held in custody until the trial – something Flora was very relieved about.

The bell above the door tinkled and dragged Flora from her musings. As she turned to welcome her first customers of the new week, the smile was wiped from Flora's face when she saw the grave visages of detectives McArthur and Blackett.

"Mrs. Miller," Blackett said, his only greeting.

"Watch out! Hide it all!" Reggie screeched, swooping down and landing on Flora's shoulder, hardly helping the tension of the moment!

"Detectives, can I get you a drink?" Flora asked, as the sombre pair hovered just inside the doorway. She had the sudden thought that they might be taking her in for more questioning, and had to fight back a sense of panic and despair. To give herself time to calm her nerves, Flora made a point of walking Reggie back to his perch, where he rather reluctantly jumped off her hand, but not before shouting "Not that jerk!" at Blackett for good measure. Flora ran her hand through her hair, which she had styled in its neat, long bob for the reopening of the place, and turned to face her rather unwelcome visitors.

"Thank you, yes a coffee would be good," McArthur replied, taking a seat at the table next to the door. Blackett followed, somewhat reluctantly, and Flora breathed a sigh of relief that this indicated they weren't here to take her anywhere.

"So," McArthur began when Flora had joined them with lattes for herself and McArthur and a glass of water for the dour Blackett, who had turned his nose up at the offer of a hot drink despite the chill of the November day, "So, as time progresses, and with no body, this has two implications for the investigation into the disappearance of your ex-husband."

"Oh?" Flora's answer was non-committal.

"Yes, first it means that we cannot pursue an investigation into a violent crime as we cannot prove that one has occurred. And second, the more time that elapses with no sightings of Mr. Temple or any bank activity or the like, the more likely it is that something sinister has happened to the man. I appreciate that these two outcomes might seem contradictory. Suffice it to say, that our hands are tied."

"I see," Flora wasn't sure where this was heading.

"Some other facts have come to light, in the course of our investigation, which we wanted your input on," McArthur continued, "if you wouldn't mind, Mrs. Miller?"

This new conciliatory tone was a surprise, and to be honest, put Flora on her guard just as much as their direct questioning at the station. Nevertheless, she managed a half smile and nodded.

"It would seem," Blackett began speaking in his usual clipped tone, "that Mr. Temple's ex-girlfriend is the new beneficiary of his life insurance policy, replacing you on the document. Presumably he hadn't had time to take her name off between the breakdown of their relationship and his disappearance."

"This does shed another light on things, as you can imagine," McArthur continued for him, like some strange and uncomfortable tag team, "and we were wondering if you could tell us anything about her character? Did you know her when she was your husband's personal assistant?"

"About her character? You mean, something other than the fact she's a marriage wrecking floosy?" Flora tried to keep her true thoughts in check.

"Ah, well, yes, did she seem reliable, trustworthy and the like?" McArthur continued fastidiously on, though the expression on her face showed she knew she was fighting a losing battle on this front.

"Well, you can trust her to steal your partner and your home, but only if they can afford to keep her in the manner to which she's become accustomed," Flora replied sardonically.

"We're getting nowhere here. I told you it would be pointless," Blackett muttered to his partner.

"Anyway," McArthur ignored him, "what about the business partner then? Jeremy Hampton. He visited us in the station … several times, and seemed very keen to find Mr. Temple. He seemed to have a… personal, more invested interest in the case, shall we say."

"Well, on that count, I suppose I can help you," Flora began, before going on to recount what she had heard of the man's phone conversation the previous week.

"Now, that is interesting," Blackett sat up straighter, his beady eyes gleaming with renewed malice, "very interesting indeed." He stood up abruptly to leave, like a hound who has found a scent and is compelled to track it immediately.

"Oh, okay," McArthur said, casting him a sideways frown and gulping down the rest of her coffee, "thank you, Mrs. Miller, you have been very helpful. Please stay available in case any further evidence comes to light."

By 'evidence' Flora presumed she meant a body, but was so relieved that they were leaving, she pushed from her mind the fact that in the detectives' eyes she was still very much a suspect. They simply had no crime to pin on her... yet. Never mind, with Blackett now chasing the wronged business partner angle, it would at least keep the pair off Flora's back for a little while. She felt slightly guilty for dropping Jeremy in it, though she had simply relayed exactly what she had heard without embellishments, but Flora decided that the odious man had probably brought it on himself. She had always suspected that he had some shady dealings of his own in his portfolio – he and Gregory really were almost a carbon copy of each other.

"Good riddance to bad rubbish!" Reggie shrieked – another of his previous owner's delightful phrases – as the detectives left and Flora sank back down into her chair. Although she felt slightly defeated by the whole situation, she was down but not out. No choice but to keep on plodding on and hope the whole thing resolved itself with no more input from her.

TWENTY-THREE

The Marshall girls appeared at the tearoom with their mum, Sally, when the older two were finished school for the day. It had become their Monday afternoon treat of hot chocolates with marshmallows and cream, though it had completely slipped Flora's mind this particular week. The place had been very quiet after the detectives had left, however, and Flora was glad to see their flushed cheeks and cheeky grins as they pulled off scarves, hats and gloves, scattering them as they rushed to say hello to Reggie.

"Welcome to the tearoom! So cosy!" Reggie chirped happily, preening himself under all their attention.

"Mummy says Reggie had an adventure like the ones in your stories, Miss Flora," Evie, the most outspoken of the three girls, exclaimed.

"Well, I didn't put it quite like that!" Sally interjected, blushing, "Sorry, Flora, I wasn't sure what reason to give for why they couldn't visit last week, I…"

"No need to apologise," Flora smiled at Sally, then turned to the girls – two pairs of little blue eyes and one pair that was green – looking at her expectantly, "Yes, he did indeed! Shall I make the drinks and then I can tell you all about it? Would you like to look through some book catalogues while you wait? I can give you each a pen to put a big circle around any that you think I should stock in my new shop."

Sally mouthed 'thank you' as Flora busied herself getting the catalogues, whilst Reggie hopped onto the table and waddled across to little Megan, nuzzling her with his head.

"It tiggles!" she giggled, and the sound warmed Flora's heart. She loved being a part of community life like this, and it was one of the main things which gave her the impetus to keep going with her plans for the converted stables.

As the girls drew circles, stars and triangles around

nearly every book on every page, in some kind of rating system that only they understood, the two adults chatted about the new Knit and Natter group in the village, run by Jean and Sally, and also about the arrangements for Billy's funeral which was to take place that Friday.

"Billy's son, Michael, has come up from Cornwall, with his son, Dave who looks to be in his forties," Sally whispered, as they tried to keep their conversation away from eager little ears, "and he is clearing out the cottage. The other son, Christopher, is flying back from America for the funeral, so they told my James, when they came to discuss the service with him."

"It's so sad they didn't see him one last time, that they couldn't have visited more often when he was alive," Flora said, though she understood that finances and life in general often stopped people from doing what they otherwise would. She certainly wished that she had taken time out of her busy London schedule to visit her own parents more often before they had passed away.

"I think the church will be packed on Friday," Sally said, understanding what Flora had meant, "and they will see how well loved he was."

"Indeed," Flora noticed then that the girls were getting

wriggly and so the women stopped talking to allow Flora to tell the story of Reggie's latest escapade – birdnapped by a mad scientist who wanted to rule the world.

"Like in Despicable Me?" Evie asked.

"Um, well…" Flora had no point of reference.

"It's a film. An animated film," Sally helped her out.

"Oh! Yes, quite so, quite so!" Flora rushed on and soon had the girls on the edge of their chairs as they wanted to know how Reggie had escaped.

"A doggy?" Little Charlotte asked, and it was so nice to hear her speak up that both Sally and Flora beamed back at the usually shy girl.

"Indeed! Tina the Tiny Terror, a canine superhero! And her best friend, Frank the ah, the ah..," Flora wracked her brain to think up a superhero name on the spot, "Frank the Feisty Fido! Yes, that's it, they rescued Reggie and brought him home."

"And the evil villain's plot was stopped?"

"It was," Flora took a deep breath and waited for their verdict.

"Yay!" All three girls clapped and Flora was relieved

that the story met with their approval.

As the family bustled out the door to go home for their evening meal, Flora's phone pinged twice in quick succession. The first was another email from Harry, this time with photos of the Captain's Dinner on board the cruise ship. The second was a text message from Lily asking Flora if she'd like to pop up to the farm that night for a meal and to do some baking. Christmas cookies, this time.

Flora, who had been trying to keep as busy as possible for the past few days, accepted quickly, before remembering that Monday was tripe night up at the farm. She couldn't really back out now, though, and resigned herself to eating as little as was politely possible. The message triggered something else in Flora's brain as well, however, and that was the memory that she was meant to 'feed' the Christmas cake so that it would be ready for Betty's return. *Oh no, the cake*, Flora thought miserably, it having completely slipped her mind in the flurry of recent events. Tidying up the dishes and cleaning down the tearoom as quickly as possible, Flora rushed home with Reggie to add the double amount of brandy to Granny Lafferty's prize-winning legacy, hoping that Betty wouldn't be able to tell that Flora hadn't quite kept to her strict schedule.

Flora left Reggie alone for the first time since his return, to drive up to the farm that evening. It was dark and too cold for walking, Flora had decided, though Lily laughed when she told her this and said that things would get much colder in this area of the country as the winter progressed. Flora shuddered at the thought, and was glad to be indoors. The table was set for two, as Lily explained Stan was at a meeting of the Local Farmers' Union. His sheepdog, Bertie, had taken the man's chair by the open fire, and Flora smiled at the homely scene. The farmhouse smelled of roasted chicken and herbs, making Flora's stomach rumble.

"I hope you don't mind," Lily said, when Flora had been divested of her coat and scarf and had a hot cup of tea placed in her hands, "since it's just the two of us, I thought we could have some soup and crusty bread. Stan will be put out if I have the tripe without him, so I'll save that for tomorrow."

Flora tried not to look too gleefully relieved as she noted the other woman's apologetic expression, "Oh, Lily, that is a shame, but I'll look forward to having it another time," Flora fibbed.

"Perfect, well now, tell me all about what's been

happening since I saw you, and how you managed to find your little bird," Lily spoke as she pottered in the kitchen, putting the homemade cock-a-leekie soup in a pan on the hob to heat through.

Flora relaxed back into her chair and enjoyed the easiness of Lily's down-to-earth company. The two women laughed together as they remembered Flora's first visit for a scone lesson, when Lily had been worried that the former city dweller would ruin her expensive clothing. Today, Flora wore a slightly smarter variation of Lily's own outfit of black jeans and a sweater. Her designer clothes had either been given away, sold, or squished into her wardrobe for future use – even though Flora couldn't really foresee when those occasions would be. Perhaps when the big house was ready? For the first time in her life, Flora realised, she felt comfortable in her own skin, and that was worth much more than money could buy.

TWENTY-FOUR

Flora was onto her third Christmas cookie with hot milk when the doorbell rang. Fresh from the bath, having spent a lovely evening with Lily, the last thing she either expected or wanted now were surprise visitors.

"Shut yer face! Shut yer face!" Reggie shrieked, annoyed at being awoken from a pre-slumber snooze.

"Hush!" Flora said, as she walked cautiously along the narrow hallway, peeking out through the spy hole in the front door to see who was on the front step. Her heart sank when she saw Phil standing there, his hair – and, indeed, his appearance in general – wild and unkempt as per usual, the only difference being a striped scarf which he had wrapped around at least half of his face, so that only his eyes and forehead were left uncovered. Flora looked down at her own attire, as he rang the bell again. Determined to be well prepared for the coming winter months, Flora had bought the thickest, thermal pyjamas she could find online. This particular set sported a rather fetching polar bear motif which covered every available inch of material.

Seeing no choice but to answer, as it was only half past eight after all, and he would have seen her car outside, Flora pulled the door open with a flourish, assuming an air of confidence which she did not feel. *Fake it till you make it*, she told herself, standing there in nightwear which had certainly never been intended for public viewing.

Phil himself seemed to be unsure whether to be shocked or bemused, and Flora caught him looking her over before quickly averting his eyes and stammering out, "Flora, ah, hello."

"Hello, Phil."

"Yes, hello, ah, I wonder if I might have a quick word?"

"Well, I was actually just settling down for the evening..," Flora began, just as there was the blur of green wings and a small bird landed on Phil's head, screeching "the fool has arrived!"

Somewhat wary, after what had unfortunately (though rather humorously) landed on Gregory's head, Flora scooped Reggie up quickly, tapping his beak to ward off another outburst. The chill night air whooshed past her and into her small home, making Flora think she had no choice but to invite the man in so that she could shut the door soundly once again and retain what little heat was left.

"Come in, Phil," Flora said, on a sigh, really having no idea what the man could want this time.

"Thank you, yes, I'm sorry to call so late," Phil jumped in with his explanation before they had even reached the sitting room, "I meant to come round earlier, but I got held up at school. Anyway, I've been feeling awful since that day I saw you at the police station, Flora. I just want to apologise. I mean, I only told them what I saw, but still, I felt like I'd dropped you in it."

"Oh, I see, well, to tell you the truth, Phil, I was in a similar position recently, having to give the police an account of a rather incriminatory phone call which I heard. I felt guilty too, even though I can't stand the man concerned, so I can empathise."

"Really? Thank you, Flora, that is a weight off my

mind. This is a small village, and although we started out well, I think there have been some… misunderstandings," Phil chose his word carefully, "that have set us on the wrong track. I would dearly like us to be friends again, if that would be agreeable?"

Flora's first thought was whether the man had an ulterior motive, and she felt immediately guilty for jumping to such a conclusion. Her mind had certainly become a lot more suspicious since moving to the village and meeting Adam – by necessity, but even so.

She tried hard to not let anything show in her expression and simply replied, "I would like that, yes."

"Perfect!" Phil clapped his hands together once, his eyes shining and his smile beaming, "I would love to help out with getting the bookshop set up, if you'll let me?"

"Well, it will be January before I get to that stage but yes, that would be lovely," Flora feigned a yawn and thankfully her guest took the hint.

"Anyway, I'll get out of your way," Phil said, eying Reggie who had taken to flying loops of the room, "and I'll pop into the tearoom over the school Christmas break to discuss it with you."

"Thank you, Phil," Flora stood, and Reggie flew to her shoulder.

"Secrets and lies! Secrets and lies!" the bird squawked in Flora's ear and she wondered – not for the first time – if he was perhaps a very good judge of character after all.

Flora stood in the kitchen of the church hall later that week, washing dishes from the wake following Billy's funeral. A strange sense of déjà-vu washed over her as she recalled doing this very thing after the service for poor Ray. This time, it wasn't Harry by her side doing the drying, but Tanya, Shona and Amy.

"Many hands make weightless work," Tanya said happily, and the other women smiled, not wanting to correct her. Considering it was her second language, Flora thought that Tanya's command of English was amazing.

"They certainly do," Shona replied, "have you had any more photos from the blissful honeymooners, Flora? Another couple of weeks and they'll be home!"

"It's funny you should mention that!" Flora said, drying her hands and grabbing her phone from the window sill beside her. She showed them the latest three emails and the women all oohed and aahed at the beautiful scenery and at the couple's adorable expressions.

"What I wouldn't give to go on a holiday like that right now," Tanya remarked, pulling her thick black cardigan closer around her. Adorned with black feathers to match her hat, it was quite a striking look, Flora thought.

"You and me both," Amy said, "I can't bear the cold. You have no idea how hard it is cutting hair when your fingers are freezing! I have to wear fingerless gloves! Gareth calls me his little icicle."

The women laughed at that, and Flora added to the anecdotes which followed by telling them about her delightful new collection of pyjamas! After Billy's sons had been in to thank them for their efforts with the food and refreshments, Flora left the group to go back to her little bird, and to remember the man who had quickly become her friend.

TWENTY-FIVE

As December arrived and the rain of November was replaced with sleet and some snow, Flora was happy to spend her days cocooned in her little tearoom, the heating blasting and Christmas tunes on the radio. Reggie, too, seemed happy that they had fallen into a rhythm and happily welcomed the customers who made their way up the hill for George Jones' mince pies, and Lily's Christmas pudding and custard from the farm shop. There had been no more visits from Adam's colleagues, and Adam himself was a constant and caring presence in Flora's life. She wasn't sure what the future would bring – and certainly didn't want to jump into anything too quickly – but what they had made her smile and, since Adam felt the same, that was enough for now.

Rehearsals for the talent show were progressing apace, and Flora had been helping Tanya with stage management and props. To be held on a makeshift stage in the church hall, Flora had the idea to offer vouchers for the tearoom to the winner. Ordinarily, the pride of coming first was considered prize enough, but Flora felt that 'sponsoring' the event might raise the café's profile in the village, especially as the event was attended by folk from the surrounding areas too. Flora was providing hot mulled wine and mince pies for the occasion and had sent out a few invitations, including one to Lizzie the pet portrait painter.

"So, Flora, what shall I put you down as?" Tanya asked, a sparkle in her eye, as they all filed out after the penultimate rehearsal.

"Sorry?" Flora was confused

"Your act?" Tanya had a smirk on her face, and Flora couldn't tell if she was fully joking or not.

"Ah, ah, I'll have to let you know," Flora blushed. A talent show was about as far out of her comfort zone as you could get nowadays – as much as baking had been before she came to the village! But she did have an idea, which she had set in motion when speaking with Billy's son before the funeral, and Flora hoped it would go down well with the villagers.

"Yes, think on it! I have left space for you in the end place, big finale!" Tanya said, as she wrapped up in her floor-length, yellow padded coat that distinctly resembled a sleeping bag.

"Oh no, I don't think that's..!" But Tanya had already headed outside into the icy night, leaving Flora flustered. She had hoped to sneak in the middle of the acts, where she could be easily forgotten, not at the end of the show where people would be expecting something grander. Never mind, she hoped the content of her performance would take pride of place, rather than the middle-aged woman who performed it!

The day finally arrived for Betty and Harry's return, and Flora was not ashamed to say that she had missed her friends. Collecting them from Newcastle airport with Adam, to avoid the older couple having to get a taxi the long way back to the village, Flora couldn't believe how well they both looked.

"Betty! You look fabulous! The sun must suit you."

"Aye lass, but I'm ready to get back to my cottage and my little dog, and I want you to fill me in on everything that has been happening while we've been away – even the little things!"

"Oh, well, I want to hear all about your holiday first," Flora stalled for time, "so let's wait till we're sitting down with a cuppa, shall we?"

"Alright then, but think on I want all the gossip!"

"Of course, of course," Flora mumbled as Adam loaded their cases into the boot. A shared look of concern passed between them, but nothing was said. Flora didn't relish the prospect of telling Betty and Harry that one of their oldest friends had passed away, and had rather wished she could leave it to the vicar to tell them. Of course, she knew that wouldn't be fair, and it would be better coming from her – especially as Betty would want all the details, and Flora had been present at the time – but still, it loomed over Flora the whole drive back to Baker's Rise. Even the winter scenery, in its sparse white beauty, was overlooked as she twiddled her fingers in her scarf anxiously.

"I'm making a slide show of all our holiday photos, so I hope you'll both come round over the holidays to watch it with us?" Harry asked, as they drove up Front Street.

"Of course," Flora replied absentmindedly.

"And how's that Christmas cake faring?" Betty asked, as Harry unlocked the door to the cottage to let them

Absence Makes the Heart Grow Fondant

all in, "I hope you've been feeding it?" Flora had let herself in the previous evening with the key Harry had left her, and stocked their fridge with a few things like milk, as well as making sure they had enough teabags for their return, so there was no excuse but to stay and share a drink with the couple.

Feeling slightly like a chastised child, Flora replied, "Yes, just as you said, and it's waiting on the table in the kitchen for your inspection!"

"Grand lass. Can you pop around tomorrow and we'll ice and decorate it?"

"After the tearoom, yes, that would be lovely."

Shona arrived as they were speaking, with Aaron and little Tina in tow. Seeing Betty, the dog launched herself from Shona's arms and towards her owner, with the older woman only just catching her in time.

"Aw there's my bonnie baby, come and give me a cuddle," Betty snuggled her face up to the little dog.

Glad of the distraction and the potential delay in having a difficult conversation, Flora said, "Why don't you stay for some tea and cake, Shona? I've brought some things down from the tearoom that needed eating, so there's plenty to go around."

As they all filed in, Shona raised questioning eyebrows in Flora's direction, and Flora knew exactly what she referred to – whether the couple had been told about Billy. Flora answered her with a slight shake of the head, before affecting her most chipper voice, "I'll put the kettle on, Adam will put your cases in the bedroom, and we can all have a sit down!"

Young Aaron proved to be a great distraction, chatting about what he hoped to receive from Father Christmas, and his part in the school Nativity production. As the second shepherd, he said he only had one line, but it didn't matter as at least he wasn't the donkey. They all laughed and agreed with him, with Harry reminiscing that when he was a boy the whole village had joined in acting out the Nativity story in the grounds of the church. The happy interlude was just what Flora had needed, and by the time Shona and Aaron left, she was ready to share her sad news. Adam had had to leave after a quick coffee, as he was on duty that evening – though Flora knew he regretted not being able to offer her some support – so she was on her own with this one.

"I see you left your car here, so at least you don't have to walk home since Adam's gone in his," Betty said, not very subtly, as they waved the others off.

Flora understood it was the polite time for her to leave, but she really needed to have this conversation, "Actually, Betty, there has been a bit of other news in the village if you'd like to hear it now? The rest I can fill you in on when we work on the cake tomorrow."

"Oh?" the older woman's ears pricked up.

"Yes, ah, shall we go and sit with Harry by the fire?"

"If you like, lass," Betty could tell there was something up now.

"So," Flora said, when they were all sitting down, two pairs of expectant eyes fixed on her, "so, there's no easy way to tell you this, so I'm just going to come out and say it, but old Billy has passed on." Flora felt the familiar lump form in her throat as she said the words.

"Oh no," Betty's face fell.

"Well, he was getting on, and ready to be with his Mabel," Harry consoled.

"Yes, but ah, it wasn't that simple..," Flora began as she recounted the sad tale of Billy's demise from beginning to end, including little Tina's part in finding Reggie's feather. By the end of her account, there was not a dry eye in the house, and it felt as if a blanket of melancholy had settled over them all.

"Aw my brave little Tina! But I never did like that Joe Stanton," Betty said, her face hardening, "a wrong'un from the beginning. Not right for this village at all."

"Aye," Harry agreed, "he's better where he is. Thank goodness they found him. Poor Billy, and the funeral already done and dusted weeks ago, so we can't even pay our respects."

"I knew you'd feel that way, and I'm so sorry," Flora felt awful, "but I didn't want to spoil your holiday with the news."

"Aye lass, we understand," Betty said, trying to discreetly wipe her eyes.

"I'm having a plaque put on his bench in the rose garden, up at the big house, and you're welcome to sit there anytime, if you like," it was the only ray of happiness Flora could offer them right now.

"That's a kind thing to do, lass, he did love that garden," Betty said, as she and Harry began to share memories of the man and his wife.

It was a while later when an emotionally drained Flora arrived back at the coach house, and remembered that she hadn't even told them about her own woes with her ex-husband and the police. That would certainly wait for another day, though. For now, a small green bird and a soak in the bath beckoned.

TWENTY-SIX

The next evening, as promised, Flora slipped and skidded her way down to Betty's cottage to finish decorating and icing the Christmas cake. The paths were a mixture of ice underneath and fresh snow on top, and it was all Flora could do to stay upright. She stopped in at the pub first, as Shona had wanted to show her the place now it had seen a fresh lick of paint and been decorated for the festive season. It was having its grand opening on Friday evening, after the talent show, and Shona hoped that everyone would leave the church hall and come straight to the Bun in the Oven to share in some Christmas carols and a few warming drinks. It looked beautiful and Flora was impressed with what Shona had achieved on a limited budget.

Absence Makes the Heart Grow Fondant

"You're going to be a great landlady, the customers already love you," Flora reassured the young woman, for whom opening nerves were now setting in, "and you can come to me for advice any time you need."

"Thank you, Flora, I hope I can do my Dad proud."

"You already have," Flora whispered, as the two women shared a hug.

The fairy lights which festooned the buildings around the village, along with the Christmas trees twinkling in windows, brought joy to Flora's heart and she smiled to herself as she knocked on Betty's front door, admiring the festive wreath which had appeared there even since the couple's arrival home the previous day.

"Get yerself in lass, you'll freeze yerself to death out there!" Betty ushered her in with her usual fussing, and Flora enjoyed the feeling of being mothered for a moment.

"Thank you, Betty. How are you doing? I should imagine you have a mountain of laundry to catch up on."

"Well, they were very good on that big ship, but no one wants to hand their unmentionables over for washing by strangers, do they? No, I brought mine home to do!"

Flora smiled and they headed into the kitchen to get on with the task of the day – icing and decorating Granny Lafferty's Christmas cake.

"Is Harry not helping?" Flora asked, as Betty began to put on her apron, all the while looking reverently at the cake which sat in the middle of the kitchen table.

"Harry? No lass, this is a job for the women of the family, I've sent him to the spare room to read for a bit," Betty spoke so seriously, with not a hint of sarcasm, that Flora didn't like to remark on how many male chefs there were nowadays. Besides, she had been included in the title 'family' and that brought a warm glow which Flora allowed herself to bask in for a moment.

The counter was laid out with a pot of homemade jam, some marzipan, already kneaded into a ball, and a large lump of fondant icing.

Betty spoke while she got a small pan out of the cupboard, added a generous amount of the jam and a splash of water to it, and then set it on the hob to heat, "This is to stick the marzipan to the cake," the older woman explained, "and while it's heating through, you can tell me why you've lost weight and permanently look like you've seen a ghost. Don't think that just because I'm old that I'm going blind!"

"I wouldn't suspect that for a minute!" Flora laughed, though inside her stomach rolled and she wasn't sure how much of the Gregory situation she should tell her friend. In the end, she opted for an abbreviated version of the truth, explaining simply that her ex-husband had tried to worm his way back into her affections, most likely for a share of the estate funds, and had since gone missing without trace. She neglected to mention the fact that she had been – and perhaps still was – the top suspect in the case, and also how many times she had been questioned by the police. It would only cause worry, and Flora didn't want to be the reason for Betty losing her post-holiday glow.

"Aye well, he clearly didn't know a good thing when he had it," Betty sniffed in disapproval of the man, "to let you go in the first place – it was his loss, lass."

"I know, I know. I'm much better off out of the marriage and out of London. Now, what do we do with this marzipan here," Flora tried to deflect the conversation back away from herself.

Betty was in her element, showing Flora how to spread the heated jam over the cake, then to sprinkle some icing sugar onto the scrubbed wooden table and roll out the marzipan, before laying it carefully over the jam.

"Now, some people leave it to dry out for another few days at this point," Betty explained, "But Granny Lafferty wasn't a patient woman, the feeding of the cake she could manage, because every time she added the brandy she took a tipple for herself, but by this stage in the making process she just wanted the cake done! Having eight children under your feet will do that to you!"

Flora laughed, "Wow, yes, I can imagine!"

"So," Betty continued, "we want the fondant icing to lie flat on the cake, and look much neater than this here marzipan, so we'll use a piece of string to measure the top and sides of the cake, to make sure we get the right size of icing. Now, you start kneading the fondant, and I'll do the measuring."

Flora did as instructed, desperate not to make a mistake, even though in reality there weren't many ways she could ruin the creation at this point. When the icing was rolled out on more icing sugar and laid over the cake (the marzipan having been brushed with water first) Betty showed Flora how to flatten it down. Flora was in no doubt that she was watching an expert at work, as Betty's nimble fingers belied her age.

Absence Makes the Heart Grow Fondant

"Now," Betty said, "we must remember that the fondant icing is merely the background, the stage on which the main decorations will sit. We don't want it to stand out in its own right, so it must be perfect, no lumps or bumps."

"Umhm," Flora said, though she was no longer listening. Something had triggered in her brain and it had begun its whirring thing, "actually Betty, do you mind if I just pop through and see Harry, you're almost done here. I'll be right back before you show me the decorations you've got for the top."

"Oh! Okay then lass, but be quick. Placing the little woodland scene is the best part."

"Of course, just a couple of minutes, I promise!" Flora quickly removed her icing-sugar dusted apron and rushed through to the spare bedroom, which Harry was now using as a study. She knocked politely and waited to be called in, all the while hopping from one foot to the other impatiently.

"Harry, you know you mentioned we could watch the slide show of your holiday pictures over Christmas, well do you mind if we have a quick flick through just on your computer screen now? Particularly those from the Captain's dinner when you and Betty were doing the waltz."

"Really? Now, lass? I thought you and Betty were in the deep end of Christmas cake production?"

"We were, we are, I just really need to see those pictures and I deleted the emails from my phone, the files were so big."

"Oh, okay then," Harry seemed perplexed, but he put down the book he was reading and fired up his computer. Each second that the now-obsolete machine took to turn on and to load up was agonising for Flora. She made a mental note to get him a new laptop for his business work as soon as possible.

"Do you mind if I sit down?" Flora asked, moving to the swivel chair in front of the desk, next to the armchair which Harry had been occupying when she entered.

"Not at all, now let me see… here they are, the pictures from the dinner. I've put them all into files you see."

"Excellent, very organised," Flora mumbled as her attention was now solely focussed on the photos on the screen. *Please, please let it be,* she said to herself, as they both watched the pictures scrolling across in silence.

TWENTY-SEVEN

"Aha!" Flora tapped the mouse to pause the stream of photographs and squinted at the screen. Even without rushing to get her reading glasses from her handbag she could see the truth. There, in the background, and enjoying a cigar and what looked to be a glass of whisky, was Gregory, with Ginny on his arm, both dressed to the nines.

"What is it dear?" asked Harry worriedly.

Flora quickly filled him in on Gregory's disappearance whilst simultaneously walking back to the sitting room to grab her phone.

"No! And you think that's him, in the background of my holiday photo?"

"I don't just think it, Harry, I know it!" Flora said triumphantly, fishing around in her purse for the card with the contact details which McArthur had given her.

"Well I never!" Harry exclaimed.

"What's all this fuss?" Betty asked, wiping her hands on her apron as she emerged from the kitchen.

"It faded into the background, just like you said the icing would!" Flora said cryptically, "But somewhere in the depths of my befuddled brain I must have noticed."

She began speaking excitedly into her phone, as Harry and Betty looked on still rather startled by the whole turn of events.

"Thank you so much for taking so many photographs, and for sending them to me, Harry, I'm looking forward to that slide show," Flora said, as she grabbed her things to rush back to the coach house where the two detectives were meeting her, "Can you resend me the email with that particular set of pictures, so that I can give the police a copy?"

"Of course, dear," Harry said, casting a worried glance at his wife who looked like she was about to burst.

Absence Makes the Heart Grow Fondant

"But what about the cake decorating? This is the best bit!" Betty exclaimed, "The little reindeer are waiting!"

"Tomorrow, I promise," Flora kissed the older woman on the cheek and rushed into the freezing night air, for once finding it invigorating.

"Well, this individual does seem to match the photos of the man which Ms Pendlebury-Muse provided," Blackett said, though Flora could still detect an undertone of disbelief and suspicion in his voice. They had zoomed in on the background in the photograph in question and all three were now studying it closely.

"And you yourself are one hundred percent certain?" McArthur added.

"Absolutely," Flora said, her cheeks flushed from relief and her slippery run up the hill. Reggie snuggled into her neck, watching the whole scene with interest. Other than an outburst of "Visitors! Visitors with money!" when the two detectives arrived, he had thankfully been calm and silent whilst they looked at the photos on Flora's laptop.

"We will need to follow this up, Mrs. Miller. Thank you for your help," McArthur said graciously, whilst

Blackett simply scowled.

"So, you think they had never broken up in the first place?" Adam asked, as they shared a cosy moment by the fire an hour later. He had just finished work and come straight over when he read Flora's urgent text describing her discovery.

"Well, it looks that way," Flora mused, "I'm guessing that he thought I'd be a pushover for his affections if he pretended that he and Ginny were no longer together, and he'd cast her aside for me. That he could get some money out of me before running away with her to escape his business debts. When I didn't comply with his plan, Gregory had to think on his feet. Apparently faking his own death and framing me for an apparent murder were next on his list."

"Then, when his supposedly ex-girlfriend told that lie about you having been in the car at the time of the crash, that muddied the waters of the investigation even further," Adam added, "as well as coming up here and batting her eyelashes at Blackett. What an awful pair. You've no need to worry now though, love, they'll get to the bottom of it back at the station."

"Thank goodness. I was so sick of having that hanging

Absence Makes the Heart Grow Fondant

over me. If only my necklace hadn't fallen off into his car. But, one last thing, how was Gregory's blood on the passenger seat?"

"Well, he could have honestly hurt himself, a nose bleed or such like, but I think it's much more likely that he cut his hand slightly so as to leave the fluids deliberately," Adam shook his head in anger, "and to have put you through all this, I hope for his sake that I never get my hands on the man."

"It's done with now," Flora leaned over and kissed Adam's cheek, cupping it with her hand, "thank you so much for believing in me, and for all your support."

"I never doubted you, love," Adam kissed her properly then, and Flora felt the remaining tension drain from her body.

"Get out of it! Sexy beast!" Reggie squawked from his perch.

"Is he going to do that every time I kiss you?" Adam asked ruefully, as he pulled away slightly.

"Um, well, I guess we'll just have to do it more so that he gets used to it!" Flora said with a twinkle in her eye.

"Now, that's a plan I can go along with!" Adam grinned.

TWENTY-EIGHT

Flora stood on the stage in a navy cocktail dress adorned with sequins and looked out over the assembled audience of locals. Her earlier nerves were gone, and she held the sheet of paper with hands that were now only slightly shaking. The clack-clacking of Jean's knitting needles could be heard in the background, where she sat off to the side of the stage proving that she could knit a little hat during the talent show. Flora had already sidestepped the little presents which the farm animals – Lily and Stan's contribution to the show and the act before her – had left littering the stage. Now she stood there, alone, all eyes and ears

Absence Makes the Heart Grow Fondant

focused on her. Flora cleared her throat once and began.

"This poem was written by our late friend Billy Northcote, for his wife Mabel. He had planned to read it out tonight, and I am honoured to be able to do so in his place.

When the skies turned black and the bombs dropped, the world gone mad with hate,

You came from the city, a girl evacuated, to find a safe place.

Like sun through the clouds, or the first rose of the season, you lit up my life

And my happiest day was when you became my wife.

Life and its seasons passed as they must,

But we battled on together, with hope and trust.

The roses bloomed, then petals fell,

But we stuck together come heaven or hell.

Until the day you were there no more,

Gone to a better place, to be with Our Lord.

Yet the roses still bloom in memory of you,

As I wait impatiently for my call to come through."

There was not a dry eye in the house when Flora reached the end of the poem. Indeed, she struggled herself to read the last verse, so overcome was she with emotion. It was certainly a fitting tribute to both Billy and Mabel, and Flora was glad to have been able to share some of his last words with everyone.

That said, Flora certainly needed the glass of red wine that Adam got for her when they were finally ensconced in the newly opened Bun in the Oven. The place was packed, with most of the folk from the talent show having walked the short distance along Front Street to support their local pub. A huge Christmas tree stood in the corner, dressed in garlands and baubles, and an open fire roared in the grate just to Flora's right, keeping her snuggly in her dress which, ironically, had originally been bought for a dinner on a cruise with

Gregory years ago.

"I can't believe it!" Shona said, as she passed on her way back to the bar from delivering some hot food to another table, "So many people have come out to support us!"

"I knew they would," Flora said, happy for her friend, "You deserve every success here Shona. Your dad would be proud!"

Shona moved away, her face blushing with pride and pleasure and the carols began then, with Harry playing the old piano in the corner and everyone joining in with 'O Come all Ye Faithful'. Edwina Edwards voice could be clearly heard, an octave above all the rest.

"I'm surprised she has any voice left after her strangled rendition of 'Ave Maria' earlier!" Adam chuckled, and Flora snorted into her wine glass. That had certainly been a memorable moment in the talent show – more of a lowlight than a highlight though!

"So, are you both coming to us for Christmas dinner, then?" Betty asked, from her spot on the table next to them.

"Don't you want to be just the two of you for your first Christmas as a married couple?" Flora asked.

"At our age? No, if Billy's passing has taught me anything, it's that we don't know how many Christmases we'll have left. I, for one, intend to celebrate each one as fully as possible!"

"Oh, well in that case, what do you think Adam?" Flora smiled.

"I say yes please," Adam replied, "if given the choice of Betty's cooking or yours..?" he winked and Flora gave him a dig in the ribs.

"Cheeky! But he's right Betty, and I can think of nothing better than spending the day with you and Harry."

"Excellent, lass, excellent, I'll get the board games out for the afternoon."

Flora cast a surreptitious grin in Adam's direction, and he wiggled his eyebrows in return. The wine was going straight to her head, but she didn't care. It was Christmastime, she was loved and had found her place in this little community, and there was everything to look forward to in the coming year. Especially so now, as McArthur had called that morning to say that Gregory had been apprehended coming off a flight from Florida. Silly fool had done all that travelling with his own passport and not a fake name. Flora didn't have any sympathy for him though, and pushed the man from her thoughts. He was very much part of her old life and she had a new life now.

A thin covering of Christmas snow lay over the wooden bench when Flora arrived on Boxing Day morning with a thermos flask of tea to keep her warm and a large slice of the very boozy Christmas cake, to say a toast to her old friend. She cleared a seat with her gloved hand, and sat down, the cold penetrating straight through her winter coat and into her trousers, but Flora didn't care.

The small, shiny plaque which Flora had had made and affixed to the bench seemed to glow in the low winter sun and Flora rubbed the water from it gently. The rose garden was sparse and somewhat bleak now, but it didn't matter. It retained a warmth in Flora's memory, from the man who had tended it so carefully for most of his adult life. Flora knew she would need to hire a new gardener in the springtime, even though the thought filled her with no joy, and she felt like she was betraying Billy. It would be more of a betrayal though, she decided, to not keep the place looking as good as he had, and so she resolved to find someone to do just that.

Billy had found simple pleasures in a simple life and Flora dearly hoped to do the same. She was looking forward to the opening of her bookshop in the new year, to seeing the big house slowly renovated and redecorated, and to hopefully launching her books into the world, all from the cosy vantage point of her little tearoom. None of which were simple goals, but Flora hoped that once they were accomplished, things could quieten down a bit.

Yes, as she thought back over all that had happened since her arrival in Baker's Rise, Flora anticipated a much quieter life in the coming year. There would perhaps be a holiday or two on the horizon, and certainly time spent with Adam, but with no visits from his dour colleagues. She didn't even want to hear the words 'death' or 'disappearance' for a long time to come!

Join Flora and Reggie in **"Muffin Ventured, Muffin Gained"**, the next instalment in the Baker's Rise Mysteries series, to see whether a quieter life is, in fact, on the horizon!

R. A. Hutchins

Muffin Ventured, Muffin Gained

Baker's Rise Mysteries Book Four

Publication Date 10th February 2022

The much-anticipated fourth story in the Baker's Rise Mysteries series brings more of the cosy humour and quaint village life which make Baker's Rise such a special place to visit!

Still reeling from the events of the past few months, Flora is keen to focus on her latest project – extending the tearoom to add a cosy bookshop with a mini library.

In the hope of enticing a famous local illustrator to collaborate on her new children's book, which features her gorgeous, feathered sidekick, Flora invites them to have the honour of cutting the ribbon at the bookshop's grand opening.

Unfortunately, it seems ceremonial scissors can bring with them dangers no-one anticipated!

Packed with humour and suspense, colourful characters and a sprinkle of romance, this next Baker's Rise Mystery will certainly leave you hungry for more!

(Includes a Muffin recipe!)

R. A. Hutchins

ABOUT THE AUTHOR

Rachel Hutchins lives in northeast England with her husband, three children and their dog Boudicca. She loves writing both mysteries and romances, and enjoys reading these genres too! Her favourite place is walking along the local coastline, with a coffee and some cake!

You can connect with Rachel and sign up to her monthly newsletter via her website at: www.authorrachelhutchins.com

Alternatively, she has social media pages on:

Facebook: www.facebook.com/rahutchinsauthor

Instagram: www.instagram.com/ra_hutchins_author

Twitter: www.twitter.com/hutchinsauthor

R. A. Hutchins

Absence Makes the Heart Grow Fondant

OTHER BOOKS BY R. A. HUTCHINS

"Counting down to Christmas"

Rachel has published a collection of twelve contemporary romance stories, all set around Christmas, and with the common theme of a holiday happily-ever-after. Filled with humour and emotion, they are sure to bring a sparkle to your day!

"To Catch A Feather" (Found in Fife Book One)

When tragedy strikes an already vulnerable Kate Winters, she retreats into herself, broken and beaten. Existing rather than living, she makes a journey North to try to find herself, or maybe just looking for some sort of closure.

Cameron McAllister has known his own share of grief and love lost. His son, Josh, is now his only priority. In his forties and running a small coffee shop in a tiny Scottish fishing village, Cal knows he is unlikely to find love again.

When the two meet and sparks fly, can they overcome their past losses and move on towards a shared future, or are the memories which haunt them still too real?

These books, as well as others by Rachel, can be found on Amazon worldwide in e-book and paperback formats, as well as free to read on Kindle Unlimited.

R. A. Hutchins

Printed in Great Britain
by Amazon